Dear Reader,

What is more appealing, more enduring than
"Cinderella," "Beauty and the Beast" and
"Pygmalion"? Fairy tales and legends are basic
human stories, retold in every age, in their own way.
Romance stories, at their heart, are the happily ever
after of every story we listened to as a child.

That was the happy inspiration for our 1993
yearlong Lovers & Legends miniseries. One book
each month is a fairy tale retold in sizzling
Temptation-style!

January brings Kristine Rolofson's *The Perfect
Husband,* a warm and witty modern-day version of
"Snow White." Heroine Raine Claypoole has locked
herself away and it takes a very special sexy Prince
Charming to reveal that she holds the power to wake
up to love. Of course, he has a few problems staying
awake himself!

In the coming months we have stories from
bestselling authors including Janice Kaiser, *Wilde at
Heart* ("Beauty and the Beast"), Leandra Logan,
The Missing Heir ("Rumpelstiltskin"), and Glenda
Sanders, *Dr. Hunk* ("The Frog Prince").

We hope you enjoy the magic of Lovers & Legends,
plus all the other terrific Temptation novels coming
in 1993!

Birgit Davis-Todd
Senior Editor

P.S. We love to hear from our readers.

A Note from Kristine Rolofson

When my editor said the words "once upon a time" I knew right away I had to write about Snow White and the seven dwarfs.

Later on, struggling to juggle the many characters in the book, I questioned my sanity in choosing this particular fairy tale. But hovering near the brink of insanity is nothing new to a writer *or* a mother of six, so I would escape to my foolproof remedy: a hot bath and a bowl of chocolate chip ice cream. I had to lose eight pounds after I typed The End.

Why did I pick "Snow White"? First of all, I thought it would be a challenge to write a romance with seven children and a not-so-wicked stepmother. And it was.

And second, I'd always wanted to do a book about a foster mother. In the past few years, I've met many foster parents. Their patience and energy are unending, their optimism a necessary ingredient in healing a child's pain. After years with a wonderful foster mother, my two youngest children entered our family with their arms open for hugs and their hearts ready to trust a new mommy and daddy. I will be forever grateful.

The location for *The Perfect Husband* was also a natural choice. Nearby Newport, Rhode Island, has always been a place where the princes and princesses of society spend their summers, and is the perfect island setting for a romantic fairy tale. In the middle of writing this story, I was so overcome with romance (and so overwhelmed by the kids) that I packed a suitcase, hired a baby-sitter and kidnapped my unsuspecting husband for a weekend at Newport's Hotel Viking. The man was so thrilled he gave me what I've been wanting for years: a laundry chute.

My married friends laugh when I tell them the name of my latest book. After all, everyone knows there's no such thing as a "perfect husband." But a man who can saw a hole in the bathroom floor sure comes close.

I hope you enjoy my fairy tale. It was written with love and a firm belief in the miracle of happily ever after.

The Perfect Husband

Kristine Rolofson

Harlequin Books

TORONTO • NEW YORK • LONDON
AMSTERDAM • PARIS • SYDNEY • HAMBURG
STOCKHOLM • ATHENS • TOKYO • MILAN
MADRID • WARSAW • BUDAPEST • AUCKLAND

For my seven "dwarfs":
Ben, Will, Nancy, Lisa, Tony and Deirdre—
and of course, Charlie

Published January 1993

ISBN 0-373-25525-X

THE PERFECT HUSBAND

1

STANDING on her front porch was easily the most handsome man Raine Claypoole had ever seen in her twenty-eight years. Even through the fine mesh grid of the screen door and despite the dark sunglasses that topped his finely chiseled nose, Raine could tell that "tall, dark and handsome" stood on the worn floorboards of her front entrance, waiting for admittance.

"Yes?" she managed, ignoring the dog that growled near her ankles. "Can I help you?"

Tall, dark and handsome smiled, and Raine blinked. "I'm sorry I'm late," he said in a low voice.

Charlie yapped at her heels. "Quiet, Charlie!" Raine continued to stare at the stranger. He wore beige slacks and a white dress shirt that was unbuttoned at the top, as if he'd whipped off his jacket and tie to combat Rhode Island's latest heat wave. It was two o'clock in the afternoon, and as far as Raine was concerned, no one was late for anything. What was this man talking about? "Late?"

"You know how planes are," he said patiently before slipping the sunglasses off and tucking them, folded, into his shirt pocket. His hazel eyes looked bloodshot. "And there was a mix-up with the car rental."

Car rental? Raine figured she must be missing some small, crucial detail that would help her understand why this man stood on her doorstep. Ready to protect his mistress and poised to attack, Charlie growled. Raine picked him up. All nine pounds quivered with repressed fury directed at the man on the other side of the screen door.

"I'm sorry," Raine began, "but I—"

"That's all right. The directions were excellent, by the way. Look," he said, flashing another smile. "It's about one hundred and ten degrees out here. I'd like to get settled and cool off."

Raine tried again, glancing at the latch on the door to make sure it was securely fastened. "I'm sorry, but I don't know who you are."

"What?"

"I don't know who you are." She raised her voice over the dog's growls. "And I don't know why you're here. I think there's some mistake." The mistake had been in answering the door. She'd planned to spend an hour napping. Jimmy had had another asthma attack, and the sibs' social worker was due to return the children within the hour.

The man took a step back and glanced at the side of the door. "219 Berkley Avenue, two blocks off Bellevue?"

"That's right, but—"

"And is this the Claypoole house?"

"Yes. And you are?" she asked, fascinated despite the possibility that he could be a robber or worse. He could have read her mail to know her name. Or looked in the phone book.

"Alan Hunter."

"I don't know anyone by that name. Who exactly are you looking for?"

He frowned. "I don't understand this. Claire said she'd taken care of everything."

"Claire?" A feeling of dread started to take root in her stomach.

"Claire Claypoole. Is this the Claypoole residence?" At her nod, he brushed the hair away from his damp forehead and continued. "Could you please get Raine Claypoole for me? I'm sure she can straighten everything out."

The dread expanded. "I'm Raine. What does this have to do with Claire?"

It was his turn to look uncertain. "She arranged for me to rent the rooms on the third floor."

"That's impossible."

He held her gaze, his hazel eyes unblinking. "No, it's not."

"They're not even her rooms to rent."

"Wait right here," he ordered unnecessarily. She watched him go down the porch steps to the sidewalk, where he opened the passenger door of a large black sedan. He retrieved a briefcase, slammed the car door and headed back up the walk to the porch.

"It's okay, Charlie," she told the anxious dog, patting his fluffy coat. "You're a good watchdog."

The man was close enough to hear the last of her words and the corners of his mouth twitched. He set the briefcase upon a wicker chair and snapped it open. He flipped through several sheaves of paper, then pulled one from the pile. "Here," he declared. "This should straighten everything out."

If this had to do with her stepmother, then the man was indeed either unrealistic or an optimist. "What is it?"

"My rental agreement."

"Hold it up to the screen."

Raine scanned the words until she realized what Claire had done, to the tune of five hundred dollars a week. *Five hundred dollars a week?* "That's a lot of money."

"Yes. It includes two meals a day." He returned the paper to his briefcase and snapped it closed. "Now, could you show me upstairs? I've had a long day."

He wasn't the only one. "She has no right to rent you anything, Mr. uh, Hunter."

"You'll have to tell her that. I paid three weeks in advance. If you have a problem I'll call my lawyers—*after* I unpack and drink a couple of gallons of ice water."

She almost felt sorry for him. Alan Hunter really did look hot. His face was red, with perspiration running from his temples to his eyebrows. "How do you know Claire?"

"My mother," he said, coming closer to the screen, "is Claire's best friend. Maybe you heard of her—and I hope to hell you have—Edwina Wetmore Hunter?"

Raine groaned. She couldn't help herself. "Yes, I've heard of her. I've even met her."

He took his wallet from his back pocket and flipped it open to reveal a driver's license. "See? Alan Wetmore Hunter. That's me."

She squinted at the photograph, blurry behind the plastic. He was who he said he was. Claire would have some explaining to do. "All right," she said, unhooking the latch on the door. "You can come in."

"Good," Alan said, but turned away. "I'll bring in my luggage."

She wanted to tell him to leave it, that he wouldn't be here long enough to change his clothes, but he was halfway down the walk before she could open her mouth. For a big man he moved fast. She continued to hold Charlie in her arms, knowing the little dog would take every opportunity to dash through the open door and run down the street to look for other dogs to play with.

Within minutes Alan Hunter arrived back on the porch with three leather suitcases and a light suit jacket draped over his arm. Raine opened the screen door, despite the feeling that this was wrong. Totally wrong.

"Where to?" He looked expectantly toward the wide mahogany staircase that graced one end of the foyer.

"I'd prefer to call Claire before you start unpacking," Raine said, setting the dog down. He trotted over to Alan's feet and sniffed tentatively.

"You can talk to her all afternoon—I don't care. I just got in from London, drove from Boston in this heat and have been awake for the past thirty hours." He still held the bags above the polished tile floor. "Show me to my rooms and we'll work out any problems in the morning." His tone implied he didn't anticipate having any problems to work out.

"You might want to leave the bags, or just take one."

"Why?"

"You're staying on the third floor," she said. "It's quite a hike. And you may want to see what you've spent money to rent before you actually move in."

He set two bags down, although he looked at her for a long moment as if he were going to be tricked.

"They'll be perfectly safe," she assured him. Raine knew when she had to retreat. She didn't want a strange man in her home, but on the other hand, she didn't want an angry strange man in her living room, calling his lawyers and making a scene. Despite his bloodshot eyes and rumpled hair, Alan Hunter looked as if he still had the power to make a very big scene.

"Will this dog bite me?"

"No."

He allowed Charlie to sniff his pant leg, but he didn't bend down to pet the animal. "What is it?"

"Part Pekingese, part Lhasa apso."

Instead of following her down the hall, he turned into the oversize living room, known as the front parlor in Aunt Gertrude's day. The tall, shaded windows rejected the afternoon sunshine, and a floor fan hummed from one corner. Two new sofas faced each other, a scarred pine table between them. Building blocks lay scattered across the black-and-white-tiled floor and baskets of plastic toys lined one wall. A low shelf behind it contained colorful cardboard books made for pudgy hands and curious minds.

Raine kicked some blocks out of her path. "Be careful," she warned. "I haven't had time to clean up the mess today."

"I didn't know you had children."

"I'm a foster mother. Claire didn't mention it?"

"No." Charlie hopped onto a faded, overstuffed chair and curled up, satisfied that the stranger meant no harm.

"Well, there's a lot she doesn't mention," Raine said, then concealed a sigh. Her stepmother would have a lot of explaining to do, but first she had to get this man out of her way. There was laundry to finish, and maybe even a tiny nap to be sneaked in, before the kids returned from camp and Mindy arrived with the sibs.

"This is quite a house," he attempted.

"Yes. I inherited it from my aunt several years ago. I really love it."

"It must have been something in its day."

"Yes," she agreed politely. She supposed she would have to give him a tour of the rest of the house now. He followed her through the parlor and into the large dining room. The house possessed a Victorian lushness that Raine had always loved, which was probably why Gertrude left it to her when there were plenty of other members of the family panting after the prime piece of Rhode Island real estate. Most of the furniture was white, painted the same color year after year in thick layers. The walls and high ceilings were a soft eggshell, the floor tiled in black-and-white squares like the living room. Oriental rugs of museum quality still adorned the floor, though not with the same vibrancy as in Gertrude's day.

"How long have you lived here?"

He was trying to be polite, Raine decided, so she responded in the same tone. "Three years. I've always loved Newport."

"Yes," he said. "I know what you mean."

She preceded him into the large kitchen, glad the doors to the utility rooms were closed. A screened door led to another narrow, covered porch. Dark pine cabinets lined the walls, and a heavy wooden table took up most of the room.

Raine led Alan out of the kitchen, figuring he'd had enough of touring her house. Around the corner, fronting the main hall, was an alcove that contained the servants' stairs. She pointed to the dark wooden staircase. "That's the servants' staircase, the only way to get to the third floor."

"I thought there was a staircase at the front door."

"Yes, but it only goes to the second floor."

He turned to follow her up the stairs. "You said you were a foster mother?"

"Yes."

"How many children do you have?"

She hadn't expected the question. "Six right now, but one of them is going to be adopted soon."

"*Six?*"

She looked back at him. "I'll bet Claire didn't mention that, either."

"No," he muttered. "She sure as hell didn't tell me I'd be spending my vacation in a foster home."

"I'm sure you could call Claire and get a refund."

"I'm not going anywhere today," he growled.

They turned a corner onto a landing, and Raine stopped. "Do you need to rest?"

"No."

She thought he did. His face was even redder than before, and she could see the dark circles under his eyes. "Are you sure?"

"Positive."

The next landing should have opened onto the third floor, but Raine had installed a door to keep the children away from the third floor. They used the main staircase, which was less confusing for her. From her bedroom downstairs, the original library, she was able to hear if the children were awake and roaming around the house.

Alan breathed heavily behind her, so Raine paused once more. "We can stop if you want."

"No," he said. "The sooner I get upstairs, the sooner I'll be settled in and the sooner I can be in bed."

Well, that was clear enough. Raine shrugged, then turned and continued up the stairs. She was used to climbing—up and down all day long, but by the time they reached the third floor, Alan was huffing and puffing and mumbling under his breath.

"Here we are," she said, stepping into a dark hallway. "These rooms haven't been used in a number of years. Sometimes my brother stays here, but he hasn't been in the States much this year."

"Neither have I."

Raine peered into one of the rooms. "You can take your pick, Mr. Hunter. There are three or four bedrooms and a bathroom. There's a tub, but no shower."

"The first room will be fine."

He stepped into the room and set down his suitcase and briefcase on the wooden floor. "What about a phone?"

"There's a separate line up here. Quentin—that's my brother—had one put in two years ago."

"I assume I can use it?"

"There are quite a few things we need to talk about. For instance—"

He put up one hand as if to ward off her words. "I'm serious, Ms. Claypoole. I am ready to collapse."

Raine studied him. "I can believe that, Mr. Hunter."

"Then you understand that talking will have to wait until I can actually absorb the information you give me. Until then, I would like to be left undisturbed."

What did he think she was, the bellman at the Hotel Viking? "No problem," she replied, and turned to leave him.

"One thing," he called, as she took a step down the stairs. "Is there air-conditioning?"

"No."

He sighed. "I should have guessed."

"I'd be glad to—"

He'd already turned into his room, so Raine didn't finish the sentence. She would have given him one of the fans from downstairs. The third floor was too stifling and dusty to be comfortable. If she'd known Claire had pulled one of her tricks and let the rooms, then she'd have cleaned them up. She hadn't expected company. Quent's band was touring Europe and wouldn't be back in the country until October. Claire always stayed with friends on the rare summer weekends she appeared on the island.

Raine heard Alan Hunter opening windows and silently wished him luck. She had to get in touch with Claire and find out what was behind her stepmother's deceit.

"I THOUGHT he'd make the most *lovely* husband for you."

"The most lovely husband," Raine repeated flatly.

"Why, of course. I've only met him once, but Edwina says he has magnificent shoulders and a charming way with women."

Raine almost laughed, but checked herself. She didn't want Claire to think that her plan was acceptable. Besides, she didn't know if they were talking about the same man. "I haven't seen any of the charm, Claire."

"You will, darling, I'm sure of it."

"I don't *want* to. Never mind. I've seen the rental agreement, though. What did you do with all of that money?"

There was a sigh. "Don't make me explain, dear."

"You have to. I'm stuck with this guy if you don't give the money back."

"I can't, darling."

"Why not?" Raine heard Alan walking through the dining room heading toward the kitchen, so she stretched the telephone cord as far as it would go, around the corner and into a small, white-tiled bathroom.

"I spent the money."

Raine made a conscious effort to stop gritting her teeth. She took a deep breath. "Claire! You have plenty of money. Why are you turning into a landlord—and it's not even your house to rent?"

"I told you, he'll make the most lovely—"

"Husband," Raine supplied, unwilling to hear the word spoken by Claire once again. "I know. Where's the money?"

"Your sofas," Claire said. "And that nice redwood play set with the swings and slides and sandbox."

Raine could hear Alan taking the stairs, one at a time. "It was supposed to be a loan." She could probably return the couches; after all, they'd hardly been here two weeks. But the swing set was cemented in. The workmen had dug nice neat holes and filled them with cement so that the swings would be safe to play on and not tip over. She'd been pleased with the precaution. Until now.

Claire interrupted her thoughts. "All the money from your mother's trust fund goes to supporting that old wreck of a house—"

"It's not a wreck."

"You're so stubborn, never letting me use your dear father's money—God rest his soul—to buy you things. So I used your money."

"*My* money?"

"The money you made from renting the upstairs. Isn't this nice? Now you don't have to pay me back."

Raine slumped against the bathroom wall, feeling the cool tile through the thin T-shirt. "Let me make sure I have this correctly. You lent me the money for the couches and the play set, then rented the upstairs to a strange man—"

"Not a strange man, dear, but Edwina's only son."

Raine ignored that. "A strange man who paid you in advance—"

"I would have just given him the rooms to use, but Edwina pointed out that he wouldn't like that." Claire sighed. "I understand he's rather independent."

"And then you took the money and paid yourself back, for me."

"Isn't this a relief? We understand each other."

"Yes, Claire. We do."

"Now you take good care of him, darling. He's a very important man, some kind of banker with investments or something complicated, like your father. See? You have *so* much in common. Edwina and I are *so* pleased."

Well, Raine was glad someone was pleased. She didn't know whether to laugh or cry, so she hung up the phone and made herself a tuna fish sandwich.

Alan entered the kitchen, this time carrying a laptop computer case and a garment bag. "I'm going to need air-conditioning."

"I'm afraid we don't have any."

"I must insist."

Raine was hot, tired and backed into a corner. "Look, Mr. Hunter, this latest heat wave is unbearable, but I can't produce an air conditioner. The fact that you're here in my house has taken me by surprise, so could the two of us just make the best of it for now?" He didn't answer, but simply looked at her as if she had four heads. "I'm asking you, Mr. Hunter. Could you stop acting as if I'm the bellboy and you're renting the penthouse?"

"I think so, yes."

"Thank you." She pushed the heavy black hair away from her face and tucked it behind her ear. She could feel her bangs plastered to her forehead. "Take the fan in the dining room. There's a pitcher of lemonade in the refrigerator. Please help yourself whenever you like."

"I'm going to finish unloading the car."

He clearly meant, *As long as I'm settled in, the harder it will be to remove me.*

Raine thought of her new couches and the children's play set, and attempted civility. "You brought your computer. Is this a working vacation?"

Alan grimaced. "Aren't they all?"

He turned and went back up the stairs, still moving slowly.

Raine almost felt sorry for him, but she'd tried to offer a fan, tried to dissuade him from walking around in the heat, but he was determined to do what he wanted. Including moving into this house.

THE FRONT DOOR OPENED and Raine heard Charlie yapping at the noise.

"Shut up, Charlie," one of the boys said cheerfully. "You're so funny!"

Raine headed toward the front of the house and the noise stopped. Three children, with identical blond hair and blue eyes, bounced toward her. "We went to McDonald's, Raine!"

A tall redhead followed them into the living room. Charlie wagged his fluffy tail to greet everyone, then retreated to his chair. There was only so much activity he could stand.

"You did?"

Julie's blond hair was tied in pigtails and a chocolate smudge decorated her upper lip. She held out a crayon-shaped drinking cup. "Look what I got!"

"Wow, are you lucky!" Raine turned to Mindy. "How'd everything go?"

"We had a great time. You know Joey—he's always happy, no matter what. The other two were a little quieter than usual. I'll tell you all about it in private."

"Come on, kids," Raine said. "You can go outside and play until the rest of the gang comes home." The children ran in front of the two women through the kitchen and out the back door.

Raine turned to Mindy. "Want some lemonade?"

"Please. Their mother didn't show up for the meeting again."

"What was the reason this time?" She took the pitcher from the refrigerator and set it upon the counter.

"Nothing, of course. No one has been able to talk to her for months."

Raine's heart sank. "The kids haven't talked about their mother lately, but I don't know how they're going to react if she never shows up again."

"They asked a few questions. I tried to tell them that Mom is having a hard time."

"*Still* having a hard time, you mean."

"The boys worry about her. Julie doesn't seem to care. I don't think she remembers much about her mother."

"I don't think she does, either." Raine checked outside to make sure the kids weren't by the door. "How much more do the courts need before they do something? These kids need a home. Something permanent."

Mindy shrugged and sat down at the table while Raine poured lemonade into glasses. "We're working on it, but you know how slow the process is."

"I know." Raine knew all too well. Her three years as a foster mother had educated her in the frustrations of the legal system. "They're in limbo until the court decides otherwise, right?"

"Yes, but the kids were fine. We had a great visit, lunch at McDonald's, and some pretty good conversation."

Raine handed Mindy her drink. "Good. They were looking forward to it."

"Thanks." Mindy took a swallow of the lemonade and grinned at Raine. "Who does the car out front belong to? If your rock star brother is in town, I want to meet him."

"Sorry, but Quent isn't due in town until October. The car belongs to a friend of my stepmother's. Claire is interfering in my life again."

Mindy's smile widened. "I'd like to meet her sometime. She sounds like a real character."

"Oh, she is."

"The kids told me she sent a play set. I promised I'd see it before I left."

"Well, take a good look, because that complicated piece of wood outside means I have a tenant for the next few weeks."

"I'm glad you're finally seeing my point," a male voice said from the hall doorway. Raine and Mindy turned to see Alan leaning against the frame. "Sorry," he said. "I didn't mean to interrupt."

"That's all right," Raine said. "Mindy, I'd like you to meet the man who is renting the third-floor apartment, Alan Hunter."

Mindy held out her hand and Alan stepped forward to shake it. "I didn't know Raine had an apartment to rent. It's nice to meet you."

"My pleasure." He released her hand.

Mindy continued to smile at him. "Well, I hope you have a wonderful vacation."

"Vacation and business combined," he replied, his smile once again charming. The dark circles under his eyes did little to mar his attractiveness, but his face remained flushed.

Raine cleared her throat, making both turn toward her. "Mindy, didn't you want to see the play set?"

"Oh, uh, yes," Mindy said.

"If you'll excuse me." Alan moved toward the door. "I'm going to put my car in the driveway for the evening."

"Bye," Mindy said, smiling once again as he left the room.

"You can stop drooling now. No one would guess that you're a married woman."

"Hey." Mindy grinned and finished her lemonade. "I'm not blind. But speaking of husbands, mine promised to make dinner tonight, so I'd better get going."

"Keep me posted on the kids, okay?" Mindy nodded, and Raine stood up and pushed open the screened door. "Mindy needs to leave," she called to the children. "Are you going to show her your new toy?"

The three children came running, the twins in the lead. Joey and Jimmy shoved each other through the doorway and screeched to a halt in front of the two women.

Raine looked behind them for their younger sister. "Where's Julie?"

"Here I am." The tiny version of the twins appeared behind her brothers. "Can I take Charlie out with us?"

"Not right now. You show Mindy the swing set, okay?"

Mindy grinned again. "It must be show-and-tell at Claypoole's house today."

"I don't know what you mean."

Mindy simply chuckled. "He is gorgeous," she whispered, as Julie grabbed her hand and started to tug her toward the door. "I think you should keep him."

Raine watched Mindy and the children head out. Keep him? She was stuck with him. There was no sense in trying to force Claire to refund the man's money. Claire never did anything anyone wanted her to do, at least, not since Raine had known her. That had been thirteen years now, when Claire told fifteen-year-old Raine that she was her new mother.

"Stepmother," Raine had corrected, furious because her father, always so withdrawn and preoccupied, hadn't told her he'd remarried.

"Claire," the beautiful woman had declared. "Of course you'll call me Claire."

Raine hadn't wanted to call her anything.

But Claire's outrageous laughter and extravagant ideas had brought some sunshine into Raine's life. Her father, still putting business first, allowed Claire to do what she wished as long as it didn't interfere with his work. He gave her an allowance and she threw tasteful parties and elegant dinners, but it was her personality that drew people like a magnet, including Edwina Wetmore Hunter—Wina—mother of Alan and quite a few other children, though Raine couldn't remember how many.

Best friends Wina and Claire hatched all sorts of plots, especially now that they were widowed. They traveled, they partied, they entertained and they meddled. Until now Raine had avoided most of the meddling, although Claire had sent Charlie as a gift to "keep Raine company." She'd adored him right away.

Raine had managed to convince Claire that she could manage on her own, with the house and her job, without outside financial help. She didn't want Claire's money, and she certainly didn't want her father's. Claire could keep it. Raine had paid too high a price for her father's fortune.

Raine stood at the back door and watched the children tumble through the redwood structures. If Claire figured that Alan would make a "perfectly lovely husband," Raine knew she was in trouble. Big trouble.

"THIS IS GOING TO BE SO much fun." Claire held her glass out to the waiter. "Put another martini in here, and don't forget the olive, will you, dear?"

Her companion waved the waiter away. "Don't listen to her, Frederick. She's not supposed to be drinking."

"Oh, tosh!" But Claire set her empty glass upon the table, shaded from the glare of the Long Island sun by a blue-and-white-striped umbrella. "I thought we should celebrate, that's all."

"I'll celebrate when Alan is really and truly married."

"It's as good as done." Claire removed a compact from her purse and brushed powder onto her nose. "I'm so clever," she said to the tiny round mirror before snapping the case closed.

Edwina shook her head, and the wide-brimmed straw hat she wore tipped to one side. She readjusted it and then wagged a bony finger at her friend. "You don't know everything, Claire. You think you do, but—"

"Didn't I tell you that the Markhams would get a divorce?"

"Well, yes, but you only knew because their housekeeper told you."

"And," Claire continued unperturbed, although she frowned at the empty martini glass, "didn't I find that nice accountant for Alexandria?"

"Pure luck," Edwina declared. "Although, wasn't the wedding lovely?"

"You have to be mother of the groom this time," Claire announced. "I shall be the mother of the bride."

"And wear aqua silk?"

Claire's eyebrows rose. "Black lace."

"You can't wear black to a wedding."

"Then something red."

"Rose," her friend corrected. "It's much more tasteful."

"All right." Claire picked up her empty glass and waved to Frederick. "I insist, Wina. We must celebrate this step, and each and every step along the way."

Edwina sighed. "Alan won't like this."

"Alan will have the time of his life." Claire winked. "I promise."

HE WAS APPROACHING the landing to the second floor when he knew he was in trouble. Suddenly his feet seemed detached from the rest of his body. Black dots began to creep into his vision from the side, and he blinked to clear them.

The darkness grew.

Alan heard his heart beating, so he knew he was still alive. He felt the perspiration running down his back, in the groove between his shoulder blades. He gripped the banister and told himself that this was the last trip on these god-awful stairs in this heat straight from hell.

He could have had an air-conditioned motel room. With a bellhop and a luggage cart and cable television with remote control. That is, he reminded himself, if he'd made reservations two months ahead of time. And he would have, if he'd known there would be these kinds of problems.

Here he'd thought himself lucky when Claire suggested "her" apartment. He'd anticipated a cozy New England retreat, private and restful. He hadn't imagined carrying his belongings up three flights of stairs in the midst of a heat wave; he hadn't counted on flight delays and jet lag and a day and a half with no sleep.

Alan gripped the fan under his arm. It was his only salvation, and he planned to strip naked and stand in front of it. He reconsidered the standing part. No, he would position it so that the cool air blew onto his horizontal body while he slept.

He took a deep breath and headed for the next landing. He could do this. He could make it. His own Mount Everest, with sleep only a few minutes away.

The black dots turned into a curtain and darkness engulfed him.

2

"IS HE DEAD?" Jimmy looked at his brother as he knelt over the body of the strange man.

Joey shrugged. "Dunno."

Jimmy sniffed and wiped his nose on his T-shirt. "Is he breathing?"

"Maybe." Joey pushed Alan's dark hair away from his forehead while Julie and Jimmy watched.

"*Now* what are you doing?"

"Looking for blood."

Julie bit her bottom lip, then turned big blue eyes upon her brothers. "I better call 911."

"No, dope. You better tell Raine," Joey ordered. "Hurry up."

The voices pierced the blackness that surrounded Alan. *I'm not dead,* he wanted to explain. *I'm just very tired.*

"This is really weird, seein' a guy on the stairs," a child's voice said. "Do you think Raine knows him?"

"I dunno. I think we'd better call the police. What if he was trying to rob us or something?"

"You mean he's a kidnapper? Wow!"

Alan wished his fogged brain could order his eyes to open and his lips to move. He didn't want to be in jail when he woke up.

A vibration under his face translated itself into footsteps and a woman's voice came closer. He heard her say, "Oh, no—what happened?" before he sank back into oblivion.

Raine hurried up the stairs, Donetta and Vanessa following close behind her.

"We don't know." Jimmy sniffed again. "We just found him."

Raine knelt down beside Alan and took his wrist, feeling for a pulse. Thank God, it was strong and steady under her fingertips.

Donetta peered over her shoulder. "You know him?"

"Yes." She felt his forehead. Warm, but not feverish. "He's, uh, a friend of the family who's going to be staying with us for a few days."

"Wow! He's not a robber?"

"Or a kidnapper?"

Raine smiled, despite her concern for the man who lay on her second-floor landing. "Neither. He's a guest."

"Think he's dead?" Jimmy asked once again, hoping this time he could get an answer.

"No. His pulse is strong."

"We heard a crash," Joey explained.

Raine noticed that the dining-room fan was a few steps down. "It looks like he fainted carrying the fan upstairs."

Joey looked horrified. "Men don't faint."

"Sure they do. But just in case, I think I'd better call a doctor." She smoothed the hair from Alan's forehead the same way the boy had. "He's not running a fever, but the heat may have affected him." Raine studied the man, sprawled on the landing as if he'd fallen asleep. He didn't look like an injured person. In fact, he looked extremely comfortable, as if he thought he was in a third-floor bedroom. What had he said earlier? Thirty hours without sleep and a bad case of jet lag?

"I think he just passed out," she declared. "Maybe the best thing would be to get him into a bed and let him rest."

"No 911?" Julie looked disappointed. "I wanted to see an ambulance."

"Not this time, hon. We'll elevate his legs and put a cool cloth on his head and see what happens. Donetta, go downstairs and get a bowl of ice and a washcloth. Boys, get me some pillows off your bed." Raine unlatched the door to the second floor and carefully opened it so as not to hit Alan. When Donetta, a tall ten-year-old, returned with the ice, Raine wrapped some cubes in the washcloth and turned Alan onto his side so she could put the cloth against his head. He moaned and rolled onto his back. Still, Raine decided, it wasn't a moan of pain but more of a sigh of contentment.

The boys raced back with pillows covered with colorful pictures of football players. Raine shoved pillows under Alan's legs and waited to see if her first aid had done any good.

The children stared, waiting too, willing the stranger to open his eyes. They didn't want to miss any of the drama going on right here on the back staircase.

"You're supposed to loosen his collar," Donetta said. "I saw that on TV."

"Right." Raine looked at the white buttons on Alan's shirt and the tanned neck above it. She managed to release two buttons and discovered a thin cotton undershirt beneath the silky fabric. Crisp, dark chest hair brushed her fingertips. "That's enough," she said, pulling back. She removed the cloth and took an ice cube and ran it along his face to soothe the heated skin.

"God, that's good, sweetheart," he groaned.

"Who's he calling 'sweetheart'?" Joey asked.

"I don't know." Raine shrugged, squelching her own curiosity.

"Maybe me," Julie chirped. "After all, I'm the one who found him."

"Did not," Joey said.

"Did, too."

"Dope!"

"Stop," Raine ordered. "Let's have some quiet here."

Alan opened his eyes and blinked. "Who are you?"

"Raine Claypoole."

Alan closed his eyes again. "Never mind. I know. I'm afraid it's all coming back to me. Where am I?"

"You're on the second-floor landing. Did you fall?"

He thought about her question for a long moment. "I don't know."

"Are you hurt?"

He opened his eyes and looked embarrassed. "No. I think I simply blacked out."

"Does this happen to you often?"

He rolled onto his back. "No. This is a first."

"You'd better get some rest."

"I thought that's what I was doing," he said, his mouth turning up slightly at the corners. It was a wonderful mouth, Raine noticed. And then wished she hadn't. Claire had sent him, but that didn't mean Raine wanted a husband.

"Maybe you'd be more comfortable in a bed. Can you walk?"

"I think so."

"Good. I can't get you up another flight of stairs, so I'm going to put you into a bedroom here on the second floor."

"No—I can make it."

"Well, I can't," she said, helping him up. "You weigh twice as much as I do."

He looked at the twins. "I think my vision..."

"You're not seeing double," she assured him, still holding his arm. "Meet Joey and Jimmy. Twins."

"Thank God." He eyed the rest of the children standing around him. "Where did you all come from?"

The children looked at him but didn't answer. Raine leaned over to take his arm underneath the elbow. "Come on. There's an extra room that hasn't been filled yet."

She guided him through the doorway, with the six children following them along the hall to a nearby room. Donetta hurried to turn the bedspread down before Alan reached the bed.

"Thanks," he said, as the child scurried away. "I think I can take it from here."

Raine released his arm, glad to stop touching him. "Are you sure?"

"Yes. This has been embarrassing enough."

Julie thrust the bowl towards him. "Here."

He took it and set it upon the nightstand. "I don't know whether to drink it or stick my head in it."

Raine put the pillows upon the bed. "I'll bring you an ice pack and a cold drink."

"Please, don't bother," Alan said, sitting down on the bed. He reached down and untied his shoes. "I'm going back to sleep."

Raine shut the shades, despite the fact that the sun was on the other side of the house, then shooed the children out of the room. She edged towards the door as he peeled off his socks.

"I still think I should call a doctor."

"I saw one three days ago," he said, his hands going to his shirtfront to undo the rest of his buttons. He seemed to be accustomed to undressing in front of women.

"Are you sick?" How would she explain to Edwina and Claire that the "perfectly lovely husband" was ill?

"Not really. It's a bad case of exhaustion. I'm afraid I planned my vacation about three weeks too late. I just need some rest." He smiled, once again the charming guest. "I'll be fine in a day or two, I promise."

"All right." Raine backed out of the room, but paused in the doorway. "If you need anything, just call out. I'll be in the kitchen for a while, if you need me, and the children sleep on this floor—one of them will hear you."

"I apologize for putting you through this much trouble."

"You don't have to apologize. Just call for help if you need it."

"I'll remember."

He leaned back and closed his eyes. Raine shut his door behind her and saw the children waiting. She put her finger to her lips. "You'll have to try to be quieter," she warned. "I don't think noise is going to bother him, but just in case, keep the music down."

"What about the doctor?"

"He already went to a doctor who told him he was tired."

"Why?"

"I don't know. I think he's been really busy in London."

"What's he do?"

"Works in a bank, I think. Come on, it's time to fix dinner. Who wants to help?"

Only one hand went up.

"I do," Donetta said, her voice low.

"Well, thank you." She looked at the rest of the sweaty group in front of her. "Everyone else find something quiet to do, either downstairs or outside."

"Can we use the back stairs?"

"Okay, but only for now. Come on," she said, herding them in that direction. The fan lay where Alan had dropped it, so Raine picked it up before any of the children could trip over the cord that lay over the treads.

"Why was he takin' the fan?"

"I told him he could. It's hot upstairs." Raine hesitated on the stairs. "You go on down. Have a Popsicle—that should hold you until dinner's ready."

"What are we having?"

Raine thought fast. "Hot dogs. Now go play or I'll put you all to work. Donetta, would you set the table? I'll be down in a minute."

She went back into the hall to Alan's closed door. She took a breath and turned the doorknob, pushing the door slightly so she could peek inside. He'd managed to remove his shoes and socks before falling asleep again. He lay stretched across the bed, his shirt unbuttoned to reveal a wide, tanned chest above the deep neckline of his undershirt.

She tiptoed inside. The room was dim and stuffy. She wondered when the weather would break. The breezes from the ocean were only halfhearted, and the island sweltered, unaccustomed to the stifling heat. She plugged the fan into a nearby outlet and turned it on, adjusting it to fan air onto the bed where Alan lay asleep.

What had Claire done, sending this man into her life? Now she was stuck—oh, that wasn't very nice, but if "stuck" didn't describe her feelings, she didn't know what did—with a sick man in her already overflowing house. A house filled with kids who needed her. She didn't need anyone else to take care of, thank you very much.

And this particular "sick man" was very appealing, even though a large chunk of masculinity, unconscious in her spare bedroom, wasn't usually her idea of something to look forward to. She preferred her men standing up, capable of uttering coherent sentences, with no prior knowledge of Claire Claypoole.

A perfectly lovely husband. Claire should see Alan Wetmore Hunter now. Neither lovely nor perfect, and definitely not husband material.

Raine tiptoed out of the room and shut the door quietly behind her. She would feed the children, maybe walk them downtown for ice-cream cones this evening, then put everyone to bed. Then she would sit down and balance the checkbook and figure out if she could afford to send Alan Hunter on his way to an air-conditioned motel room.

That is, if he ever woke up.

ALAN DIDN'T KNOW where he was. He drifted out of sleep gently. There was no buzz of an alarm clock or shrill telephone wake-up call from the front desk. He stretched, keeping his eyes closed, hoping he'd figure out his location before he opened them. The light beyond his eyelids told him it must be day. Sultry summer heat wrapped itself around his skin, along with a sheet.

He didn't know where he was, but he liked it.

Once he'd opened his eyes, he wasn't so sure. The day started to come back to him—the long flight, the traffic in Boston, and the ebony-haired woman with the big blue eyes—eyes with an expression that had said she'd rather he slept on the sidewalk. The silly, fluffy dog hadn't liked him, either.

There were no other sounds except a fan. He remembered wanting the fan. He sat up slowly, jamming a pillow behind his head against the iron headboard. A heavy, ivory shade covered the window, a tall, walnut dresser sat in the alcove between the corner of the room and the closet door. Everything in the room was tall and narrow—even the mirror above the dresser.

He looked around for his suitcases and didn't see them. Then he threw back the sheet and looked down in surprise. He still wore his pants. His white shirt lay in a heap on the ivory rug that covered a small portion of the wooden floor next to the bed.

All at once Alan remembered. But none of what he remembered made the least bit of sense.

"WHAT DAY IS IT?"

Raine jumped, startled to hear a man's voice behind her. She turned to see Alan standing in the door between the laundry room and the pantry, the two narrow areas that lay behind the kitchen. "Thursday."

He frowned. "Thursday? It can't be."

"Okay." She turned back to dumping clothes into the washing machine. "What day would you like it to be?"

He stepped farther into the room. "I slept for... twenty hours?"

She shut the lid of the washer and pushed the button to start the machine. "That's right."

"I can't remember the last time I slept like that."

"You must have needed the rest."

"Yes," Alan agreed. "I suppose so." He shoved his hands into his pockets. "I remember being surrounded by children. Did that happen?"

"Yes. They found you on the stairs and then called me."

"How, uh, did I get undressed and into bed?"

Raine wanted to smile, but she didn't. "I helped you into bed. You did the undressing yourself."

"Oh."

"Disappointed?"

"Definitely." He grinned. "My fantasy life was in high gear for a while."

"Sorry."

"Where are the kids?"

"They're at playground day camp."

"I really didn't imagine them, then?"

"No," she repeated. Despite the fact that he was conscious, he was still pale. The man needed a few days in the sun. "I was just going to have lunch. Would you like a sandwich?"

He looked relieved. "I'm starving. I've been wondering if this time I'd faint from hunger."

"You should have said something. I would have brought you a tray."

"Should I clean up first?"

Raine shook her head. She preferred the unshaven, scruffy look. For now he didn't look like a high-powered banker or a perfectly lovely husband. "No."

He grinned, rubbing one hand over his cheek. "Now I know I'm on vacation."

"I thought you were in Newport on business."

"In one respect," he said, following her into the kitchen. "I have an important legal matter to clear up."

She sensed the rest was confidential, so didn't push. Instead she told him to sit down at the narrow trestle table while she made thick turkey sandwiches.

"Root beer, Diet Coke or iced tea?"

"Root beer."

She fixed an oversize glass with ice cubes and set the glass and a can of root beer in front of him, along with a paper plate filled with the sandwich and a handful of potato chips.

"Start," she said. "Don't wait for me." She slid the salt shaker and pine napkin holder in front of him, then arranged her own lunch. By the time she sat down across from him, Alan had eaten half his sandwich and all of the chips, so Raine stood up again, grabbed the extra sandwich and the bag of Ruffles and put them in front of him.

"When was the last time you ate?"

"I don't remember."

Raine could believe it. He ate like someone who had just washed up onshore after a shipwreck. She sipped her iced tea and nibbled on half a sandwich while she watched Alan empty the plate in front of him. When he'd demolished another sandwich and drained his glass of root beer, Raine attempted another question. "Do you work in London?"

"Yes. Or rather, I used to."

Either he was a very quiet man or he was very good at keeping information to himself. "Used to? Did you lose your job?"

He looked shocked. "Of course not. Why on earth would you think—?"

"Because you didn't say anything about yourself," she explained. "You don't remember the last time you ate, you don't say what you do or where you work, and you passed out on my stairs yesterday afternoon. You're very mysterious. And you must be under a lot of stress."

He leaned back in his chair and started to laugh. "I've never been called mysterious," he said, his dark eyes twinkling at her. "I have four younger sisters. They know everything about me and always have."

"Do they know why you're here in Newport?"

"I'm sure they've been told." He leaned forward. "Look, Raine, I'm sorry. We got off on the wrong foot yesterday. Maybe we could start over."

She shook her head. "You don't understand. You don't know why you're here, do you?"

"Of course I do. I paid a high sum, too."

"I'm not talking about why you're here in this house, although I guess that's exactly what I'm talking about."

"Are you going to eat that?"

Raine pushed her plate away with the uneaten half sandwich. "Go ahead."

He took it. "All right, I give up. Why am I here?"

"Claire and Edwina have decided I need a husband." Raine didn't like saying it out loud like that, but there was really no choice.

"Edwina. My mother, you mean?" He looked blank.

"Yes. A 'perfectly lovely husband,' Claire said." Men, for all their wonderful qualities, were sometimes not really very bright, when it came right down to subtle meanings.

He swallowed. "And?"

"She was describing you."

Alan choked. Raine stood up and pounded him on the back.

"Better?"

He took a deep breath and nodded. When he had himself under control, he studied Raine with a more serious expression. "She must have been joking."

"I don't think so."

"They couldn't possibly have thought . . ."

"That's why you have to leave. I can give you your money back in a couple of weeks. In fact, I can give you some of it today. I wrote a check." She stood up again, retrieved her checkbook from her purse and sat back down at the table. She ripped out the check and handed it to him.

He took it and looked at the figure. "This is only one week's worth."

"I know. It's the best I can do."

He handed it back to her. "Look, I don't want to be here if it's a big inconvenience for you. But it's July in Newport—the height of the season—and I may need a few days to find something else. I'd rather stay here. I'll even buy a small air conditioner and put it in one of the third-floor rooms because I'm tired of hotels."

Raine hardened her heart so she wouldn't feel sorry for him. "You're being set up. Whether you realize it or not, your life is no longer in your control."

He smiled. "I doubt the situation is that serious. Claire and my mother may have wanted us to meet, but I doubt that this is a full-blown matchmaking attempt."

"Not an *attempt*," she stated. "It's a scheme. A plan. A plot. And you're falling right into their hands by staying here."

He didn't look as though he understood anything. "This is the nineties. No more arranged marriages, remember?"

"Claire has it all figured out."

"We're supposed to look at each other, fall in love and live happily ever after?" He shook his head. "That's storybook nonsense, and we both know life doesn't work that way."

"Tell the old ladies. I know Claire, and I know what she's capable of doing."

"And I know my mother. She's a sweet woman who never meddles in my life."

"No? You look like a man who makes his own reservations. Why didn't you rent a room at the Viking or take a cottage for the summer?"

He frowned. "I'd planned to, until I heard about an upstairs apartment off Bellevue Avenue."

"And where did you hear it from?"

"My secretary. Who talked to my mother."

"Right. And I'll bet she made all the arrangements, didn't she?"

His expression told her she'd hit pay dirt. "This is ridiculous!" he protested.

"I'm warning you. I've been dealing with Claire's plans since I was a teenager, when she married my father. She likes to rearrange other people's lives. It's a hobby, or maybe it could be called a compulsion, I don't know."

"Why hasn't she found you a perfectly, uh, lovely husband before now?"

"She's tried."

"Well, you've managed to defend yourself so far."

"She never sent one to the house before."

"Look, you're a perfectly lovely woman yourself. And although it would be tempting to climb between the sheets with you and spend some time sampling that perfectly lovely body of yours, I don't have the time or the inclination."

"You're gay?"

"Don't look so relieved. Not *that* inclination—I'm taking about sex with a woman who lives with a bunch of kids and a dog who looks like a cat. A woman who thinks every man who knocks on her door has been sent by her stepmother to marry her." He stood up and pushed back his chair. "I really don't think you're my type."

"Thank God."

"What?"

"Then you'll leave." She pushed the check back to him. "That's great."

"I'm not going anywhere." He ignored the slip of paper. "Except downtown to buy an air conditioner for my 'apartment.'"

"Look," she began again. "Be reasonable."

"Reasonable? *Reasonable?* I've paid to live here, at least for the next three weeks, with an option for three more if I want. That includes two meals a day—lunch and dinner." He looked at his watch and then back at Raine. "What time is dinner?"

"Six, but . . ."

He nodded. "Fine. In that case, I'd better get busy. I have a lot to do today."

Raine watched him leave the kitchen and heard his steps on the stairs. She picked up the check, soggy from sitting in a puddle left by the root-beer glass. The ink ran, blurring her signature in the corner. She'd tried to warn Alan Wetmore Hunter of the danger he was in. But had he listened? No.

Hardheaded, Raine decided, crumpling the check into a ball and tossing it toward the garbage can in the corner of the room. Wasn't it just like a man to ignore the obvious dangers and rush headfirst into trouble?

3

"Just wanted you to know I've talked to my supervisor. We're pushing for a termination hearing as soon as we can get a court date."

"Thanks for telling me, Mindy." Raine tucked the phone under her ear and leaned against the kitchen counter. "You know how I feel about those kids. They were my first foster children and we've been through a lot together."

"I'll be on vacation for a couple of days, but I'm going to write up the summary report, and hopefully the judge will approve the petition the first time around."

"And then?"

"Adoption, but we'll cross that bridge when we come to it. I'm even trying to be transferred into that unit, so keep your fingers crossed for me."

"You'll have to give me plenty of warning if they're to be adopted. It's going to be hard to part with those three."

"Don't worry. They're all set with you for the time being, and we won't be in any hurry to find anything less than perfect."

"Okay." Somehow Raine didn't feel any better. The thought of saying goodbye to Joey, Jimmy and Julie made her want to cry. "I'm getting ready for the boys' birthday party. They'll all be back from camp in an hour. Lily should be back any minute—she's been visiting with her new family for the past three days."

"How's that going?"

"Great." Raine smiled to herself. "They're good people and Lily's starting to get attached to them."

"We're still set for permanent placement next week, I hear. Holly's picking her up Monday?"

"Yes. At ten."

"You going to be okay with that?"

"It's never easy to say goodbye to any of them."

"This is a tough business."

"No kidding."

"Maybe that handsome tenant of yours will be around to take your mind off things."

"Don't tease, Mindy. He's not my type."

"That's the most ridiculous thing you've ever said."

Raine chuckled. "I have to finish wrapping presents for the boys' party. They requested a picnic, so we're heading over to Ten Mile Drive."

"Well, have fun."

"We will," Raine promised. She hung up the phone and surveyed the gifts spread on the kitchen table. She'd bought two of everything, only in different colors. Three years ago, when they'd felt comfortable enough in the house to tell Raine anything at all, they'd told her that they preferred it that way. Two plastic warrior turtles, two G.I. Joe action figures, two neon bathing suits, and two green and white T-shirts with Boston Celtics splashed across the fronts needed to be wrapped.

Two of everything was what the children needed. Including two parents. Mom and Dad. She couldn't provide that, no matter what she did. At least not now.

She wasn't even dating anyone. There were no male role models around, either. Quentin was a fantastic uncle, but he wasn't here much. His rock and roll band kept making music and giving concerts.

Raine wished she could keep the three children with her always, but would that be the best thing? She knew that lots of foster parents adopted the children in their care. Half the kids in the state never made it up for adoption because the foster families kept them. But she was a twenty-eight-year-old single woman.

And the children, especially the twins, needed a father.

Raine swallowed hard and reached for the wrapping paper. She had a lot of thinking to do, but it boiled down to what was best for the children.

When Charlie barked at the front door, Raine had finished wrapping the last of the presents. The Damons, a young black couple, stood on the porch.

"Hi. Come on in." Raine opened the door and the Damons stepped inside. Lily, a chubby toddler with dark eyes and drooling grin, clung to the woman who held her in her arms.

"Did you have fun with your Mommy and Daddy?"

Janet reluctantly handed over the toddler to Raine. "I can't wait until next week. This visiting process is starting to get to me."

"I'm glad she's had time to adjust to the change," Raine said. "Remember how shy she was the first few times?"

Bob Damon set down the diaper bag on the tiled floor. "We're going away for the weekend," he announced, smiling at his wife. "Our last trip before we become parents."

"Bob tells me it will make the time go by faster," Janet added.

"What a wonderful idea." Raine winced when Lily tugged a lock of her hair. "Monday will be here before you know it. The social worker is bringing her to you, so I'll have to say goodbye now. I'm sure you and Lily will be very happy together."

Janet's eyes filled with tears. "Thank you for taking such good care of her."

"We've all loved her. We're going to miss you, aren't we, Lily?" The child giggled.

"Rain, rain," she chanted. "Go."

"You'll go next week, go with Mommy and Daddy." Raine and Lily waved goodbye to her future parents. Then Raine kissed the baby's soft cheek. "Want to go swimming today?"

"Beach!"

"That's right, angel. Won't we have fun?"

"THERE HAS TO BE a way out of this."

The young attorney, his dark hair carefully combed back from his forehead, shook his head. "I'm sorry, Mr. Hunter, but I don't think that's necessarily true."

"You're going to sit there and tell me there is no way to get around a thirty-year-old will?"

He shook his head and tapped the papers in front of him. "Your grandfather was very specific."

"My grandfather was crazy," Alan muttered.

"Not legally."

"No," Alan agreed. "Not legally. This idea must have made sense in 1959, when I was four years old."

"It's actually not all that uncommon, Mr. Hunter. My father handled many unusual cases in his day."

"Which you inherited."

The young man almost smiled. "Yes. My father retired several years ago. He's probably out sailing on the bay this very minute. Do you sail, sir?"

"No." Alan preferred to swim in the water instead of gliding on top of it. "Are there any of the original lawyers left?"

"Just Benjamin Atwater. He works one afternoon a week, to keep his fingers in the pie, so to speak."

So to speak. "That name sounds familiar."

"I believe he and your grandfather enjoyed playing golf together many years ago."

Alan leaned forward. "Is this one of those situations where my lawyers meet with you for months—maybe years—to settle this will?"

The man sighed. "I sincerely hope not. That would be a big waste of time and money for all of us, and I would rather spend my time on the bay. Why don't you talk to Benjamin? He's visiting his nephew in Wyoming for a few weeks. I can call you when he returns. Maybe he'll have an idea where we could go with all of this."

"I don't want to lose the property," Alan stated.

The man shrugged. "Your grandfather was very specific. Twenty-five years after his death, the oldest married grandson was to inherit everything. Or the estate reverts to the state of Rhode Island." He snapped the file shut.

"I'm the *only* grandson," Alan growled, "and I'm not married."

Jonathan D. Horton III spread his hands, palms up, in a gesture of surrender. He grinned, as if he'd just thought of something funny. "Then maybe you'd better find a wife."

Alan stood up, unamused by the comment. "I'll make an appointment with Ben Atwater."

"Talk to Mrs. Murray at the reception desk. She'll contact you when he returns."

"Fine." The two men shook hands. When Alan left the discreet brick building, a blast of heat hit him full force. He stood near the harbor, beside the Brick Marketplace. Across the narrow street lay the wharves and another area of warehouses renovated into shops. He was tempted to wander through the marketplace, but the heat deterred him. He hadn't forgotten the strange weakness he'd experienced on the Claypoole landing. He'd felt fine when he'd returned the rental car and walked to the lawyer's office, but the return trip was all uphill to Bellevue Avenue and Raine's house.

Disgusted with the lack of progress this afternoon, Alan shoved his hands into his pockets and headed up the hill. He'd had few illusions about easily wrapping up the legal process concerning the will. His own lawyers had warned him, but he'd decided to take matters into his own hands. He hated taking so much time from work, but he would settle the problems here—even if it took him the entire summer.

"HERE, HONEY BUN," she crooned. "It's so nice to have you back."

Alan, having entered the house without Charlie noticing, stopped in his tracks and peered into the kitchen. "What?"

Raine, kneeling on the floor beside Lily, looked up and flushed. "I wasn't talking to you."

Alan smiled. "I didn't think so." The thought of his mother trying to match him with Raine Claypoole still struck him as hilarious—as if he'd entangle himself with a woman like Raine, however beautiful she was. And all those children. He shuddered.

"How are you feeling?"

"Fine," he replied. "Mind if I join you?"

"Come on in. We're waiting here for the rest of the kids. They should be back from day camp any minute." Raine lifted the chubby toddler into a high chair and tucked a bib around her neck. "There you go, Lily May." She scattered a handful of Cheerios on the tray and the baby picked one up carefully between two chubby fingers and popped it into her mouth.

Alan pulled up a chair and sat down at the table. "Aren't you going to introduce me?"

The baby's eyes widened at the sound of the strange voice, and she craned her neck to see who was speaking. Her big, dark eyes remained wide as she assessed the stranger.

"This is Lily. She's almost one."

"Hello, Lily."

The baby picked up more Cheerios and reached toward Alan. He took a bit of cereal. "Thank you."

Lily grinned and reached again, her palm open.

"I think you're supposed to give it back now," Raine suggested.

"I realize that." He handed the piece of Cheerios back to the baby. "I happen to be an uncle."

Lily banged on the table. "Rain, rain!"

Raine put another handful of Cheerios onto the tray. "That's it until dinnertime," she stated, then turned back to Alan. "Lily is going to live with her new parents next week. She's a very lucky girl."

"Is it hard to give her up?"

Raine swallowed and looked away. "Yes, but that's part of my job. Knowing Lily is going to have a wonderful new family really helps."

"Do you really take care of six children?"

"Yep."

He gulped. "That's a lot of kids. How did you get into this kind of, uh, work?"

"I collected college degrees for a while, trying to decide what I wanted to do with my life." She smiled. "It took me a while, but I realized I loved working with children. So I became a second-grade teacher in a private school in New York, but it wasn't exactly the way I envisioned it to be."

"And?" he prompted, curious why a beautiful young woman would turn away from New York and hole up in Newport with a house full of homeless kids.

"Aunt Gertrude left me this house and I decided—in two seconds flat—to move to Newport. I applied for teaching jobs on the island and ended up substituting until one of my new neighbors suggested I think about foster care. So I trained, got my license, and have been taking in children ever since."

"How long is that?"

"Three years."

"That's a long time." Not that there was anything wrong with children. It was the sheer quantity that shocked him. Although Raine's blue eyes, silky black hair, long eyelashes and neat little body could certainly tempt a man, there were a lot of reasons to take two steps backward. Thanks, but no thanks.

"Yes, it is."

Alan looked around the kitchen as Raine began stacking food on the counter. "This place reminds me a little of my grandfather's house." He wondered if he'd ever own it. The thought of the property reverting to the state made him tighten his lips into a thin line.

"I like old houses." Raine counted the slices of bread, then opened the oversize jar of grape jelly.

"You look as if you're getting ready to go somewhere."

"A picnic," she answered. "If you really have your heart set on two meals a day, then you can join us. If not, feel free to stay here and order a pizza."

"I'll stay."

She didn't look surprised. "I can leave a couple of sandwiches for you. What do you prefer—tuna or peanut butter?"

"Tuna." He noticed the birthday cake on the counter. "Whose birthday?"

"The twins."

"The boys who thought I was dead?"

"Exactly. They're turning eight today, and having a picnic is their idea of heaven."

"I haven't been on a picnic in . . . many years."

"Your work keeps you that busy?"

He thought for a minute. "Yes, I guess it does. But I like it that way. I've always enjoyed traveling, especially in Europe."

"So, what brings you back here?"

"To the States?" At her nod, he continued. "The end of a very large project. And just in time, too." He smiled at the toddler across the table. "I have business to take care of here in Newport, and you know I needed a vacation."

"You'll have to call your mother off," she said, plopping sandwiches into small plastic bags.

"I will," he assured her.

"I've tried to call Claire, but I keep getting her answering machine."

"If she's as determined as you say she is, why bother calling her at all?"

"To tell her that you're not interested in me. She may accept that and leave you alone."

"And if she doesn't?"

"Then I have to think of a way to keep her out of Newport."

"Don't worry. My mother always spends the summer with my sister—the married one with the grandchildren—in the Hamptons."

"I hope you're right."

The doorbell rang, and Charlie barked furiously from the living room. "I'll get it," Alan offered. "I'm expecting a delivery."

Raine shot him a grateful look. "Thanks." She was too busy to wonder what he would be expecting. Some official documents, she supposed. She was amazed he didn't travel with a fax machine—at least, she hadn't seen him carry one in from his car.

"Bye, bye," Lily called.

"Bye, sweetheart," he said.

What was going on here? Busy banking types didn't play with strangers' babies. He was charming, that was certain. Claire had said he would be.

Raine opened the cupboard and took out a stack of plastic cups. She'd be glad to get away for a few hours.

The children's footsteps pounded through the house. "I'm in the kitchen," she called, but they had already burst through the door. "Hi. Did you have a fun day?"

"Raine, guess what!"

"What, Joey?"

"We had a shaving-cream fight!"

Raine set a bag of ice cubes in the bottom of a large blue and white insulated cooler. "A shaving-cream fight? With the counselors?"

Jimmy nodded. "Yeah. It was so cool."

Donetta turned up her nose. "It was disgusting. I pretended I didn't know them."

"So, what did you do while they were playing with the shaving cream?"

"I was with my friends playing the mall game."

"Oh," said Raine, suppressing a smile. "That sounds fun, too." The boys' clothes were streaked with water, their blue T-shirts grimy from playground dust. Julie, who didn't look much cleaner than her older brothers, tugged on Raine's arm.

"It was so funny." She giggled. "They put the stuff on top of their heads."

Raine bent down and gave her a hug. "Where's Vanessa?"

"Holding Charlie. The man—you know, the sick one—he's getting a present."

"He is?"

"Yep. Van wanted to watch."

Joey danced around Raine. "What about the party? Can we have our party now?"

"Sure, we can. Go put your bathing suits on, get your beach towels off the clothesline and don't forget to go to the bathroom."

"Hurray!" the boys cried. Donetta and Julie raced them out the door. Raine picked up Lily and went through the dining room to find Vanessa. A shy five-year-old, she tended to forget where she was supposed to be or what she was supposed to be doing. This time she was sitting on one of the new couches, Charlie curled up in her lap. When she saw Raine and Lily, she smiled.

"Hi, Van. I heard you had fun at camp today." The little girl nodded, her long dark hair swinging across her shoulders. Sometimes Raine thought the child looked Asian, with her dark, almond-shaped eyes and straight hair. "Charlie can't be up on the new couches, remember?"

Vanessa lifted the tiny dog from her lap and set him upon the carpet. "Charlie likes the couch."

"I know he does, but he'll lie down in his chair."

They watched as the tiny dog tossed them a dirty look and hopped into the rocker. He curled up, rested his head upon his paws and closed his eyes.

"We're going on a birthday picnic, remember?" Vanessa shook her head. "Well, we are. Go get your bathing suit on."

Alan entered the living room and Vanessa stopped short.

"Did you get your package?"

"Package?"

"Didn't you just have something delivered?"

"Oh," he said. "Yes. Who's this? Another one of your children?"

"Yes. Vanessa, this is Mr. Hunter. He's visiting here at the house for a while."

Vanessa stared at him, then hurried out of the room.

"Bashful, isn't she?"

"Vanessa's been with me for six months now, but she doesn't like to speak. I don't know if she's shy or afraid."

"Where are her parents?"

"That's anybody's guess." Raine lowered her voice. "Vanessa's mother has been in and out of prison. She's out now, but no one's seen her in months. Whenever she reappears, the state attempts reunification."

Alan sat down on the couch and Charlie came over to his feet and growled. "Why does this dog hate me?"

"I think he's just being very protective."

"Well, tell him I'm not going to touch you."

"Charlie, go away." The dog trotted off to the kitchen.

Alan put his hands behind his head. "You were telling me about Vanessa. What's reunification?"

"That's when they attempt to reunite the children and the parents—to live happily ever after."

"You don't sound convinced."

Raine hesitated in the doorway. "I get that way sometimes. Sometimes it's hard to believe that the kids will go back home and live happily ever after."

"You have a very strange job."

"You're right." She smiled. "And I have to get back to it. See you later."

Ten minutes later the children were tucked inside the minivan, along with two coolers and a paper bag stuffed with picnic gear. She'd told the boys that candles wouldn't work near the ocean, so they'd consented to save dessert until they were back home again. Raine climbed behind the wheel, slammed the door and felt as if she'd been set free.

She had been, actually. From Alan Hunter and his lethal charm. She'd met enough men like him to last her a lifetime. So many, in fact, that she considered herself immune. The Wetmore Hunters of the world were wealthy, handsome, charming and confident—and not at all the kind of men Raine wanted for a mate. She wanted a down-to-earth guy who would put the family before making money, a man who would be faithful to her and would think a recliner and a television set with a twenty-seven-inch screen were the ultimate in home decorating.

She wanted a man who'd want her—with her children and her house and her secret, silly dreams of happily ever after.

But not Alan Hunter.

"WHAT ABOUT THAT GUY?" Joey set a bag of garbage upon the counter.

"He's probably upstairs," Raine said, lugging the cooler into the kitchen and putting it onto the floor in front of the sink. Everyone was sandy and covered with salt after two hours of playing by the ocean.

"Can he come to my party?"

"I don't know," Raine stalled. Then she saw the disappointment on the boy's face. "I'll ask him, but you and Jimmy need to get into the shower right away. No cake or presents until everyone is clean and in their pajamas!"

"Aww!"

"I'll set the table and put Lily to bed and we'll be ready for a party in no time at all, you'll see." Raine took the baby out of Donetta's arms and shooed the rest of the children out of the kitchen. Lily was half-asleep, so

Raine quickly readied her for bed and popped her into the crib. The child had had quite enough excitement for one day. Then, remembering her promise to Joey, she hurried upstairs to the third floor.

The door to one of the rooms was closed, but a loud, humming sound came from behind the walnut door. It didn't sound like a regular fan. Raine knocked quietly on the door, then called, "Alan?"

In a minute she heard a muffled sound, so she called his name again.

"Just a minute," he called back. Then he opened the door; Raine opened her mouth but no sound came out. He looked as if he had hastily pulled on a pair of light khaki slacks, because the waistband was undone. His chest was covered with a mat of dark hair. His shoulders were as Claire had described them, broad and nicely defined. All in all, he did not look like a man who spent his days counting money behind a desk.

"Excuse me," she began, then felt cold air hit her face.

"Come on in," he said. "You're letting the heat in."

Her gaze went to the large appliance in the window. "You bought an air conditioner?"

"I told you I was going to."

"I said no."

"No, I don't think you did. You offered me a fan."

Raine tried to remember the conversation, but couldn't recall the exact words. "Is this what you had delivered?"

"Yes. I even had it professionally installed, so there would be no problems. I have no intention of living in an oven for the rest of the summer."

"The rest of the summer? I thought you were only going to be here a few weeks."

"It depends," Alan said. "Now, what can I do for you?"

"You're welcome to join us for birthday cake. The party is about to begin."

"Great." He reached for the shirt hanging on a hanger on the doorknob. "I'll be right down."

"You don't have to if you don't want to," she said, stepping back.

"I want to thank the kids for helping me yesterday," he assured her. "Are there any others I haven't met yet?"

"Probably, so brace yourself."

The children jumped around the kitchen, while Donetta poured punch and Julie arranged paper napkins on the table. Her little helpers, Raine thought, were always trying to make themselves useful.

"Is that man coming?" Joey asked, sliding into his seat.

"Yes."

"Great! Is he still sick?"

"No, I don't think so." Raine grabbed a box of candles and proceeded to arrange eight on one side of the cake, then started in on the other side. Eight each, so they could each blow out an equal number and declare an official wish.

"Can I blow out candles, too?"

Raine looked down at Julie. "Not until your birthday."

"In October?"

"That's right."

"Joey, sit down beside Jim and settle down."

"Move over, butt-head," the boy told his brother.

"Watch your mouth," Raine warned, standing on tiptoe to reach the book of matches she kept stashed above the stove. "And behave yourselves, especially in front of company." She turned around and saw Alan enter the room.

"Happy birthday," he said to the boys.

Jimmy grinned at him. "You didn't die, huh?"

"Not that I know of," Alan said, looking at the children seated around the table. "Aren't you missing someone?"

"Lily's in bed already. She's had a busy day." Raine pointed to a seat at the foot of the table. "Sit down and I'll let the children introduce themselves."

Alan smiled at Vanessa. "I know you, don't I?" The child simply stared at him without saying anything. Alan looked at Donetta. "You're the young lady who brought the ice pack, aren't you?"

Donetta nodded. "Yes. I'm Donetta."

"Thanks for the help." The girl shrugged, unsure of what to do around a stranger. The boys wiggled on their seats.

"We found you on the stairs and we were gonna dial 911, like the television show, but Raine came and said we didn't have to because you weren't dead and you didn't have a heart attack—"

"And you were just sleeping or else you fainted, but men don't faint, do they?" Joey interjected.

Alan looked surprised. "I'm sure they do, although maybe they don't talk about it much."

"You haven't met Julie, the boys' younger sister," Raine said. "Julie, this is Mr. Hunter."

"Call me Alan," he told the children. "It's easier."

Julie edged closer to Alan and looked up at him with wide, blue eyes. "Are you a daddy?"

"Uh, no."

Do you know how?"

"Probably. Why?"

"I need one."

"Jeez, Julie, shut your face," Joey commanded.

"Don't be such a dope." Jimmy groaned.

"That's enough," Raine warned the three of them as she lighted the candles. "We're going to sing 'Happy Birthday' now." Donetta turned the overhead lights off, then moved into a chair, then Raine set the cake upon the table in front of the boys.

"Ready?" The children nodded. So did Alan. Raine began the song and everyone joined in. When it was over, the boys leaned forward, blew out their candles in two identical gusts and grinned.

Raine wondered what they were up to. "Did you make a wish?"

"Yep."

"Yep."

"Good." She hoped it was something that could come true. Raine took her seat at the head of the table and scooted the pile of paper plates closer to her. "I'll cut the cake. Birthday boys get theirs first."

"Yay!" the boys yelled.

The next hour was a noisy combination of chocolate frosting, wrapping paper, homemade cards and spilled punch. The boys ripped the paper off their presents and exclaimed their pleasure over every gift.

Charlie paced underneath the table, hoping cake crumbs would fall. Occasionally he barked, hoping Raine would feel sorry for him and share a piece of cake. The boys donned their new T-shirts over their pajamas and insisted on sleeping in them. They loved the action figures and the plastic turtle warriors, ate two pieces of cake each and hugged everyone at the table. They were shocked speechless when Alan handed them envelopes with a five-dollar bill tucked inside each one.

Raine finally sent everyone upstairs to bed, with instructions to be quiet and not wake Lily. "I'll be up in ten minutes to tuck you in," she promised.

"That was quite a party," Alan said, leaning back in his chair. "Is it always like this?"

"Like what?"

"Chaos."

She frowned at him and stood up to clear the table. "I wouldn't call it chaos exactly. It's just, well, it's just the way it is with six kids."

"And a dog that looks like the working end of a mop."

Raine smiled, balancing a handful of sticky plates. "A very small mop." She dumped everything into the garbage can in the corner and returned to the table for another load.

"Why do you do this?" Alan stood up, walked to the garbage can and carried it back to the table. "There," he said. "It will save you some trips."

"Thanks. Why do I do what?"

"Take care of other people's kids."

"I love children. Why is that such a crime?"

"That's not what I meant. Your father was one of the richest men in New York."

"Meaning I must have a hefty trust fund that supports me, and allows me to have anything I want for the rest of my life?"

"Your father was a very successful man. I'll bet he never dreamed you'd have to support yourself by changing diapers and taking in kids."

"I don't think my father ever thought about it one way or another. Making money was the only thing he cared about."

"It's not a crime to make money, Raine."

"I forgot. That's what you do for a living, isn't it? Investments or something?"

"Yes, but—"

Raine went to the sink and grabbed the sponge. "The only thing I inherited was this house, from Aunt Gertrude. My mother died when I was a child, leaving me a small trust fund that pays the taxes and some of the utilities, but nothing else. I didn't want my father's money. I support myself," she declared, wiping the tabletop. "And I like it that way."

4

"HE'S NOT PLEASED WITH ME," Edwina told her friend. She hung up the phone and looked out the window toward the golf course. "Not pleased at all."

"He'll be fine," Claire assured her, holding out one tiny, veined hand. "Do you think I should have this ring reset?"

Wina studied the oversize gold band studded with diamonds. "It *is* slightly, mmm, showy. Are you thinking of something simpler?"

Claire put her hand down and drummed her fingertips on the glass tabletop. "I'm thinking of something quite complicated. I remember an excellent jeweler in Newport, on Thames Street. In fact, I can't possibly imagine trusting these diamonds to anyone else."

"Oh, no, you don't. I'm already in trouble with my son. He's accused me of meddling, which I've never done before."

"Not to him. But what about the girls?"

Edwina grimaced. "Daughters are fair game."

"It's different with boys?"

"Of course. They get so irritable and touchy."

Claire sniffed, obviously thinking that "irritable" and "touchy" people were minor matters to deal with. "I thought asking Alan to watch over her was a nice touch."

Edwina brightened. "It was, wasn't it? Especially when I mentioned we might have to come to Rhode Island and check up on my son's health *and* your overworked, fragile stepdaughter."

Claire chuckled. "He didn't want us descending upon him, did he?"

"Alan's a private person," his mother said. "He's always been that way."

"He's about to change, then, isn't he?"

"I don't know, Claire. He didn't sound too pleased."

"She's perfect for him. He needs livening up."

"You don't even know him!"

Claire looked at her and sighed. "Well, does he or doesn't he need some excitement?"

Edwina pretended to think about it. "He does," she finally admitted. "He's going to turn into an old man before his time, stuck in his ways, giving his entire life to his work and living alone."

"Not anymore," Claire assured her. "Everything is falling into place quite nicely."

"Do you really think so?"

"Trust me," Claire declared. She held her hand up again. "Now, what do you think? Should I change to white gold?"

ALAN SHOULD HAVE KNOWN his mother was up to something. His sisters had warned him, but he hadn't taken it seriously.

Not until now. Not until Raine.

So, the old women were now attempting blackmail. *Take care of Raine or we'll arrive in Newport ourselves.* Which didn't matter to him at all. He'd planned on visiting his family in a few months. He'd spent

Christmas in Denver with Stephanie and her brood, along with everyone else, six months ago. His mother had looked radiant and contented and only slightly curious about the women in his life.

Women. As if there were hundreds. He'd dated some interesting, ambitious women and become lovers with several. But there'd always been something missing. The women he'd met either protected their independence with savage ferocity, to the point of no compromise, or had looked upon him as the answer to their prayers, making him feel as if he had Rich Husband branded all over him.

He had no plans to be anyone's husband.

His last months in London had been hectic—he'd spent so much time flying between London and Moscow, he'd been relieved that he didn't have a woman in his life. Now he didn't know what he wanted anymore, or even if a woman with warmth, intelligence and humor existed anywhere. Especially one who could handle the jobs of hostess and traveling companion with sophistication and class.

Alan almost wished he'd continued talking to his mother. She usually made him laugh, even when she was interfering in his life. And it was only right, he decided as he headed downstairs, to admit to Raine that she'd been right all along.

"IF WE DON'T GET THERE early it's going to be too crowded, so eat your breakfast and then get your bathing suits off the line." Raine, dressed in a long shirt and sandals, handed the twins cereal bowls and spoons.

"Get where?" Alan asked.

"To the beach. You left your air-conditioned room? Your computer and your telephone? A miracle."

"For now," he admitted. "I was lonesome."

She shot him an amused look. "Right."

"Really," he insisted. "I've been working so long, I think I've forgotten what I used to do in my spare time." He looked around the kitchen at the piles of sandwiches and bags of potato chips. "Having another birthday party?"

"No. Just lunch."

"Sounds like fun," he hinted. Maybe if he spent the day with her he could report to Edwina and Claire that Raine was in good health—at least physically. The mental part he wouldn't even try to hazard a guess about.

She didn't pick up the hint. "Should be. Damn."

"What?"

"I'm out of bread."

"You must spend a lot of time in the grocery store."

"More than I'd like, that's for sure."

"I can go get you a loaf of bread, if you like."

"You?"

"Why not? Isn't there a store right down the street?"

"Yes, but you don't look like the kind of man who knows his way around a supermarket."

He pretended to be hurt, smiling at her surprise. "I've been a bachelor a long time. I didn't starve." Barely, he amended silently.

Donetta sat on the end of the long counter, swinging her legs and talking on the phone. The boys ate cereal at the table, while Lily sat in her high chair, banging her chubby palms on the plastic tray and screeching. The two other little girls were nowhere to be seen, but he heard shrieks from the backyard. Charlie didn't leap from underneath the table and growl, so Alan assumed he was outside guarding the girls.

"Thanks, anyway, but I think there's enough for lunch, after all." She looked over her shoulder at him as he poured himself a cup of coffee from the carafe on the counter. He edged carefully past Donetta's swinging feet and took a seat at the table.

"You coming with us?" Joey asked. He lifted the cereal bowl and drank the rest of the milk.

"I don't—"

"Yeah," Jimmy added. "Are you? That'd be cool."

"Well . . ." He looked at Raine. "Mind if I tag along with you?" Accustomed to a busy schedule and hectic life-style, Alan was tired of his room. Despite the frequent telephone calls from the office, he missed having adults to talk to. Going to the beach with Raine would have to do for now. He'd also get some exercise and fresh air, two things the doctor had advised.

"It could be a very long day," she said, hoping he'd say no, but hoping for the boys' sake that he'd agree to go. They didn't get much time with men.

"I need the exercise."

"True, but you may prefer peace and quiet."

"I can find a quiet place on the beach."

Raine gave up the argument. He'd learn there were no quiet places on the beach, especially on a Sunday morning in July. "Peanut butter or ham?"

"Ham. Extra mustard. What time are you leaving?"

Raine shrugged. "Whenever we get ready. Sometimes it takes longer than others."

He looked at his watch. "It's eight o'clock now. Eight-thirty departure time?"

"I don't know. We'll leave when we get in the car."

"Which should take how long?"

Raine put down the box of plastic sandwich bags and turned to face the man at the table. "Why don't you relax, enjoy your coffee, have some breakfast, and then get ready for the beach? We'll leave when we leave."

He grimaced. "I'm having trouble slowing down."

"Yes, you are."

He sighed. "This is going to be harder than I thought."

Raine almost felt sorry for him. "Well, just remember you've only been on vacation a few days. Sometimes it takes a while to unwind."

He looked hopeful. "That's true." He picked up his coffee cup. "Is this decaf?"

"No, but there's a jar of instant in the cupboard above the coffeemaker." She didn't offer to get it for him.

Donetta turned the radio on to WRX and an old Rolling Stones tune blasted from the speakers. She nodded toward Alan. "Cool oldie, huh?"

Alan nodded back. "I thought kids listened to rap music."

"I do, sometimes. Sometimes I don't."

"Oh."

Joey pushed a gaudy cereal box toward him. "You want some?"

Alan took the box and examined the side panel of ingredients. "No, thanks."

Donetta raised her voice. "I'm trying to win an hour."

He took a sip of his coffee and winced. "An hour of what?"

"Of my choice of songs—a WRX listeners' choice hour."

Raine tossed sandwiches into a paper bag. "That's why she's sitting by the phone. If she's the right caller, she wins the hour of music."

Alan looked confused, but Raine figured he'd get used to confusion if he insisted on staying here.

"What kind of coffee is this?"

"Whatever was on sale last month." She grabbed a sponge and wiped off the counter. "There," she stated, tossing the sponge into the sink. "We should have enough to eat."

Alan eyed the bags of food and the large cooler on the floor. "Yes, that looks like enough for the New England Patriots."

"You followed football in London?"

"Sure."

"You don't look like a football kind of guy."

"I played in college."

"Wow!" Joey gasped. "Can you teach us how to throw?"

"I thought you were into baseball," Raine said.

Jimmy shot her a withering look. "You can do both, you know."

"Oh, sorry." She tried to hide her smile. The boys scooted their chairs closer to Alan, who drained the rest of his coffee and looked at the half-empty carafe on the counter. As the boys peppered him with questions, Raine took pity on Alan and refilled his coffee cup.

"Thanks," he said, interrupting an explanation of a play.

"How much of this stuff are you used to drinking?"

He smiled. "Too much."

"I thought so." She replaced the carafe and motioned to Donetta. "Time to load the dishwasher."

The girl reluctantly slid off the counter and moved closer to the sink. "I can still call, can't I?"

"Sure, but while you're waiting you can do your work, okay?"

The child sighed. "I guess so."

Raine interrupted the boys. "You can talk to Alan later, guys. Go get your bathing suits and shirts on, and put your pajamas in your drawer, not on the floor."

Alan stood up and took his empty cup to the sink. "I have refrigerator privileges, don't I?"

"Of course," she said. "I can empty part of a shelf for your food."

"Good. I'll need to pick up some things."

"Are you sure you want to go to the beach with us? It could be pretty—"

"I'm sure. I need the exercise."

Exercise was not how she'd classify a morning at the beach with six children, but Raine didn't waste her breath discussing it. This was obviously a man who did what he wanted when he wanted to, and he didn't take kindly to advice to the contrary.

"I CAN'T BELIEVE how many people are here at ten o'clock in the morning." He'd forgotten the beaches. He'd grown used to swimming pools and lakes with private docks. He'd forgotten the crowds, music, lifeguards and enormous number of people.

Raine handed him a bottle of sunscreen. "Sunday's the worst day."

"Then why come?" He wished she'd take off that oversize shirt. It hung down to her knees. Very cute knees, actually, supported by smooth calves and tiny feet.

"It's fun."

"Fun," Alan repeated flatly. He looked around at the crowds of people surrounding the faded bedspread that served as command central for Raine's group. Lily, protected by a large yellow T-shirt and a wide-brimmed hat, sat in the sand, digging a hole with a plastic shovel. Vanessa, making sure she was safely near Raine at all times, sat beside the baby and helped mound hills of sand. The other four played in the surf.

Raine leaned back on her elbows and faced the ocean. "I love to watch the people."

Alan could agree with that. Many long-limbed, shapely beauties had strolled past their blanket. A few had given Alan the once-over, then seen Raine and the children. Alan figured he must look like Father Goose in sunglasses.

Still, at least he was in the process of relaxing. He would relax if it killed him. He picked up the book he'd brought and opened it at page one. Within minutes he was completely absorbed.

A shadow fell over the page. "Whatcha readin'?"

Alan looked up at Joey/Jimmy. "Nothing right now."

"Wanna swim? I know how to bodysurf."

"Maybe later."

"When?"

Alan looked at his watch. He was cornered. "How about half an hour?"

The boy grinned. "Great!"

"That was Joey," Raine stated. "In case you didn't know."

"I didn't," he managed to reply. Raine had removed her shirt and sat on the bedspread beside him in a one-piece, red bathing suit.

"He'll hold you to it, you know."

"Yes." Alan nodded, hoping his sunglasses hid his surprise. She had a lovely body—trim, neat and at the moment nicely oiled. Her black hair brushed her smooth shoulders when she turned to talk to him.

"That's nice of you. He doesn't have the chance to be around men and it's good for him." Her lips turned up at the corners and he wished she wasn't wearing sunglasses, so he could see if she was teasing him or not.

"Why?"

"You know, male role models. I'm going to enroll the boys in Scouting in the fall, that is, if they're still with me."

"Why wouldn't they be?"

She looked back to the shoreline where the older children bounced in the surf. "It depends on what the state decides is best for them. They might be up for adoption by then." Raine looked at the book in Alan's lap. "What are you reading?"

He flipped it shut so he could read the cover. *"Dealing: the Fate of American Companies in the Next Decade."*

"Oh."

"It was written by an acquaintance of mine," he said, wondering at the same time why he felt he had to defend his choice of reading material. "The reviews were excellent."

"I'm sure it's a very good book," she agreed, but didn't look at all convinced. "It sounds more like a college textbook than a beach book."

"What do you consider a beach book, Miss Claypoole?"

She turned to smile at him, then resumed watching the shoreline. "That's easy. First of all it should be a paperback. That way, if you get sand in it or it gets wet, it won't matter as much."

He tapped the glossy cover. "This isn't going to get wet."

"Oh, of course not. That's because you don't have children on the blanket beside you."

"No." He gestured toward the people on the next blanket. "I have *them* on a blanket beside me." A young man and woman lay locked in an embrace, oblivious to the crowds of people around them. Of course, Alan decided as he glanced over, he'd rather be doing something like that instead of reading a book on business deals.

"I see what you mean."

"What else?"

"It should be fiction. Something relaxing, a book you've wanted to read all winter and didn't have the time for. It shouldn't be so suspenseful that you forget to watch the kids, though."

Alan realized he enjoyed watching *her*. The tops of her breasts rounded nicely from the bodice of her suit. He'd always been partial to the color red, especially this particular cherry shade. "Of course not."

"It should have nothing whatsoever to do with what you do for a living."

"Meaning business."

"Whatever."

"The idea is to learn nothing?"

"The whole idea is enjoy yourself, to take a mental vacation."

"I guess I'll have to go to the library."

"See?" Raine sat up and helped Lily sit down on the bedspread. "You're learning how to take a vacation, after all."

"I've taken lots of vacations," Alan countered. "All over the world."

"Then why are you in such bad shape?"

He readjusted his sunglasses and stretched his legs. Lily patted him on the knee. "Hi," she said.

"Hi," he answered, hoping she wouldn't take that as encouragement to climb all over him.

"You're not answering my question."

"All right. I've spent the last ten months negotiating with the Russians and setting up several projects. It was a twenty-four-hour-a-day process, especially since we wanted to nail things down before the country self-destructed any further."

"I thought you were in London."

"Based in London." He shifted slightly so Lily could have more room.

"Are you going back at the end of the summer?"

"I don't know where the next project will be."

"Eat!" Lily cried, grabbing one of Alan's toes.

"Here, pumpkin," Raine said, reaching for the baby. "We'll have a snack."

"Uh-oh," said Alan. "Here comes the bodysurfing expert."

All four children trotted toward them, dodging between beach blankets to plop near Raine's cooler. "We're hungry," Jimmy stated, eyeing the bags of food by Alan's tennis shoes.

"May we have a drink, please?" Julie squatted near Alan and gave her older brothers a dirty look.

"Yeah," Joey said. "Please." He looked at Alan. "You promised to go swimming, remember?"

"You want to go now or have a snack first?" Alan didn't believe in breaking promises.

"Go now," Joey said, as if he couldn't risk the possibility of Alan's changing his mind in the next ten minutes.

"Okay." Alan stood up, tugged his blue polo shirt over his head and tossed it onto the bedspread. Then he removed his watch, put it inside his shoe and removed his sunglasses.

"Here," said Raine, holding out her hand. "I'll tuck them in my bag."

"Thanks." His fingers grazed hers for only an instant, but the contact of her warm skin jolted him. Alan dropped his hand quickly and turned toward the two boys.

"Alan?"

He looked back at her and thought what a pretty picture she made, sitting on the blanket. If she were anyone else, he'd attempt to get to know her better. But he already knew all he had to about Raine Claypoole, and everything he knew was a warning to stay as far away as possible. "What?"

"Don't let them go out too far," Raine said.

"They'll be fine." Alan stepped onto the sand, enjoying the sting of heat against the bottoms of his feet. Four children followed him to the water's edge, and Alan wondered just what kind of vacation this was going to be, playing male role model to such an assortment of children.

He put his hands upon his hips and four pairs of eyes stared at him. "You can all swim?"

They nodded.

"Everybody can bodysurf?"

They looked uncertain, even Jimmy, who said, "Kinda."

Great. He was responsible for the survival of four kids in the Atlantic Ocean. "Okay, here's the deal," he said, making his voice stern. "Stay with me and do as I say."

The boys nodded, Julie squealed as incoming foam tickled her ankles, and Donetta waited for further instructions, her hands on her hips, too. "I can do CPR," she said. "Just in case anyone drowns."

"I'm glad to know that," Alan assured her. "Okay, everybody into the water!"

RAINE WATCHED from the blanket, rarely taking her gaze from the five bobbing heads in the surf. Vanessa sat on the shoreline and created small mountains in the wet sand, and Lily curled up beside Raine, put her thumb into her mouth and fell asleep. Raine adjusted the umbrella so that the child was shaded from the morning sun.

She'd have gone to the shoreline herself, just to be closer, if Lily hadn't dozed off. Now she was forced to stay here on the blanket and pray that the children learned to bodysurf without drowning.

It seemed an eternity before they returned, skin dripping with salt water. Raine passed out towels and listened to the children's excited chatter.

"They did great," Alan said, slicking his wet hair back from his forehead. He looked younger that way.

She wished he'd put a shirt on or cover himself up with a towel. She handed him one.

"Thanks," he panted, and wiped his face.

There were those magnificent shoulders again. Raine watched him quickly pass the towel over that part of his body, rub his nicely furred chest a couple of times, then plop onto the blanket beside her.

She inched away.

"Sorry," he said, noting her move. "I'm getting you wet?"

"That's okay," she managed. "Thanks for swimming with the kids."

"No problem," he said. "I'm out of shape, though."

He didn't look out of shape at all. The modest black bathing trunks topped a pair of muscled thighs. "You looked like you were having fun."

"Yeah." A look of surprise crossed his face. "We had fun. I should do this every day while I'm here."

"True. It's your vacation." She opened the cooler and lifted a can of ginger ale in the air. "Thirsty?"

"Thanks." He took the can and popped the metal tab. "I don't know how much salt water I swallowed."

Raine dispersed sandwiches and poured lemonade while Donetta opened a bag of pretzels and passed it around. The older children described the length of rides the surf had given them, proudly displayed the scrape marks on various parts of their bodies and compared their prowess to Alan's bodysurfing ability, which was, as Joey put it, "Awesome."

Raine feigned shock. "Awesome?"

"Totally," Jimmy added. "For an old guy, he's pretty fast."

"For an old guy?" Alan repeated, as if he couldn't believe what he'd heard.

"Old and awesome," Raine muttered, trying not to laugh at Alan's dismayed expression. "Wow."

"I think I'll go back to my reading," he said, rummaging through the pile of clothes until he found his book. "Old guys need their rest."

"Everyone is going to stay out of the water for a while." Raine gathered up the garbage into a plastic bag. "There are apples in the cooler. Or you can wait until later on."

"When do we have to go home?"

Raine looked at her watch. "It's after eleven. How about in another hour? I don't want anyone to get sunburned."

Alan tossed the book aside. "Fine with me."

Raine looked past his shoulder at the couple beside them. No longer silently entwined, they lay face-to-face, talking to each other. She could see their lips move, saw the smile flit across the face of the young woman. She was probably twenty; her skin was tanned evenly, which meant she was probably a college student with a job working nights. You didn't get a tan like that on weekends. The young man was lighter. Raine figured if he wasn't careful he would have one killer of a sunburn by sundown.

"People watching again?" Alan murmured, leaning close so the children wouldn't overhear. "At least they're taking a break."

Raine flushed. "I wasn't—"

"No boyfriend?"

"What?"

"It's a simple question. Do you have a man in your life—such as a boyfriend, good friend, relationship, et cetera?"

Raine pushed up her sunglasses onto the bridge of her nose. "No."

"Which is why your stepmother sent you one."

"Well, she sent *you*. You wouldn't be described as a boyfriend, good friend or relationship."

"True," he conceded. "I'm the perfectly lovely husband."

Raine groaned. "I wish I hadn't told you."

He chuckled. "It's sounding funnier every time I think about it."

"They're serious, you know."

"Who—Claire and Wina?"

"Yes."

"Don't worry, Raine. I took care of it."

She looked at him curiously. "How?"

"I called my mother yesterday and told her to back off."

"And she agreed, of course."

"Of course. She's a reasonable woman." He lay on his back and shoved a clean towel under his head for a pillow. It was obvious he was getting comfortable. She hoped the kids didn't throw any sand onto him.

Raine rolled her eyes. "Claire isn't."

"I'm going to enjoy my vacation," he murmured, closing his eyes and taking a deep breath.

Easy for him to say, Raine figured. She had the sense of impending doom she always had where her stepmother was concerned.

It was a shame, Raine thought, watching him lie there in contentment, a shame that he wasn't a different kind of man—someone not quite so good-looking or rich or businesslike. Someone who had no ties to the social stratosphere or financial wizardry. She didn't mind having money—at least, she hadn't in the past, but she'd be damned if she'd spend the rest of her life with a man like her father, a man who put dollars before family and business before his children.

What on earth was Claire thinking?

5

CHARLIE SNUGGLED CLOSE to Raine's side, taking up
more space in the queen-size bed than a nine-pound dog
should occupy. She moved away from the heat of his
body, then, realizing there was no more room, gently
nudged the dog until he moved over.

Raine readjusted the sheet and heard a noise in the
hall. None of the children had been roaming around the
house lately, but nothing they did would surprise her.
Charlie began to snore, a high, wheezing sound that
made Raine smile until she heard muffled sounds from
the kitchen.

She peered at the numbers on the digital alarm clock
on the nightstand. Two-thirty. Somebody was about
to be returned to his or her bed. Charlie paid no attention as Raine stumbled out of bed and headed for the
kitchen.

The light was on over the sink, and as Raine tiptoed
through the doorway, she saw Alan standing by the
counter, holding a glass. He wore light-colored shorts—
nothing else.

He winced when he saw her. "Sorry," he said, keeping his voice low. "I tried to be quiet and not wake anyone."

"That's okay." Raine stood in the kitchen doorway
and brushed her hair from her face. Then she realized
she was wearing only a long T-shirt and crossed her

arms in front of her chest. "I thought one of the children was up."

He went to the refrigerator and took out the pitcher of iced tea. "Do they do that often?"

"No, but sometimes they have nightmares. Why are you up in the middle of the night?"

He poured tea into a glass, then opened the freezer for the ice cube tray. "I was thirsty. Want some?"

Raine hesitated. The night was sultry and her skin still felt warm from the time on the beach this morning. "All right." She sat down at the table, telling herself he'd seen more of her body in the bathing suit today than he would right now, but still felt uncomfortable wearing her nightshirt in front of a strange man.

Alan quickly assembled another glass of iced tea, even going as far as to take a lemon from the refrigerator and slice two pieces into the glasses. He left the pitcher on the counter, then sat down across from Raine and handed her a glass.

"Thanks." She took a sip. "Couldn't you sleep?"

He shook his head. "No, but I'm used to it."

"Doesn't the air conditioner help?"

"The heat isn't the problem."

"Then what is?" The quiet was incredible, heavy and peaceful, and Raine began to relax, although she wished she had thought to put on a robe. She would have to remember from now on.

He took a long drink, and the only sound in the room was the ice cubes tinkling against the glass. "It's nothing new. I usually wake up in the middle of the night and then can't get back to sleep for hours, if at all."

"Why not?"

"Too much on my mind, I guess. I made a few phone calls to the London office and ran through some numbers on the computer."

Raine wasn't surprised that Alan couldn't take a real vacation. His type never could. "I thought you were supposed to be on vacation."

"An enforced one," he admitted. "I'm supposed to rest, relax, exercise, eat sensibly and watch my blood pressure."

"And are you?"

"I've been trying, but it's not easy. I love my work." He gave her a rueful smile. His face was darkly handsome in the dim light, and Raine wondered again why he wasn't married. He seemed at ease talking to a woman in the middle of the night.

"Good luck. This place isn't exactly peaceful and quiet."

"So I've noticed."

She reached for the pile of books on the table. *Scenic Newport* was the one on top. "Are you going to do some sight-seeing while you're here?"

"Yes. I planned to sit here and make a list." He pulled a yellow legal pad from underneath the books and pamphlets and turned it around so she could read it. "I've already started."

Raine peered at the neat handwriting. "You're going to do the Cliff Walk, tour seven mansions, bicycle Ten-Mile Drive, take the railroad dinner train.... Wait a minute, there's a question mark on that one." She looked up.

"I haven't decided on the train for certain."

"Oh." She looked back at the list. "Tennis Hall of Fame. That's a good one."

"I remember being there briefly years ago."

She pushed the pad back across the table. "Sounds like quite a schedule."

He lifted it up and peered at the writing. "That's only part of it." He put the pad down again and drained his iced tea. "I might even buy a treadmill."

"You really do want to get in shape," Raine said, trying to control her smile. He was a classic Type A personality. "I thought you were supposed to slow down."

"I am."

"You're planning your vacation as if it was a battle plan. Or rather, a business strategy."

He leaned back in his chair. "How would you do it?"

"I think I'd play it by ear." When he frowned, she couldn't stop her amusement from showing. "You know, wake up in the morning and say to myself, 'Gee, what do I feel like doing today?' Then I'd go back to sleep."

"And then what?"

"When I woke up I'd think about it again and do whatever I felt like." She took a sip of her drink. "I don't think I'd worry about it in the middle of the night."

"What about you? Isn't there anything you worry about in the middle of the night?"

"Sometimes," she admitted. "But I usually don't have too much trouble sleeping."

"I can see why," he said. "Six kids wear you out."

"Five, as of tomorrow."

"What happens tomorrow?"

Raine grimaced. "Lily is going to leave in the morning. Her social worker is taking her to her new family."

He looked surprised. "Isn't it hard for you to give her up?"

Now it was her turn to be surprised. "Yes," she answered, resting her elbows on the table. "But I feel good knowing she'll have a permanent home. The people are very nice and can't wait to adopt her."

Alan nodded. "I'm glad."

"And I have two more coming in a few days."

"Two more kids?"

She nodded.

"That makes seven. *Seven*."

"I can add."

He rolled his eyes. "So much for the perfect vacation spot."

"I didn't ask for you, you remember. And I offered you a way out. You can still take it."

Alan watched as Raine stood up and walked over to the sink to put her glass there. Her black hair looked even darker, and the delicate, womanly curves of her body could be glimpsed underneath the cotton shirt. She was definitely a temptation.

"No, thanks," he answered, wishing he could take her into his arms and see how she felt beneath his hands. "I'll stick with my original plan."

She turned and smiled. "I thought you'd say that."

"How?" He stood up, studying her face in the shadowy mixture of dark and light. She was beautiful, with a heart-shaped face, large eyes and wide mouth. Funny, in the chaos that usually surrounded her, he'd noticed nothing beyond a certain prettiness.

"Investment bankers prefer to stick to plans."

He moved closer. "You have personal experience with investment bankers?"

She looked up at him with dark blue eyes. "My father. You may have met him."

"Yes. A powerful and brilliant man."

"He liked to stick to plans, too."

"There's nothing wrong with plans." Alan really didn't want to talk about her father. He wanted to bend over and kiss that little frown from her lips.

"Perhaps." She shrugged, and the movement brushed the cotton across her breasts. "Right now I plan to go back to bed."

"Good idea." He touched her shoulder as she began to move past him. "Raine," he began, wondering why on earth he'd touched her, wondering what the hell he was going to say. "Will you be all right?"

She looked surprised. "Why wouldn't I?"

"Tomorrow, I mean. You seem very attached to that baby."

"Is there something wrong with that?"

He put both hands on her shoulders to stop her from walking away. "Not unless it gives you pain."

"Pain to see her leave, joy to have been able to take care of her. It's a mixture of both."

He shook his head. "I don't know how you do it."

"You can't keep yourself insulated from pain—no one can." She peered at him closely in the darkness. "Or can they? Is that how you live—not getting involved enough to get hurt?"

"Nonsense," he snapped. "That's not—"

"It's a nice, safe way to live," she said softly. "And I don't blame you at all. But you don't have to worry about me."

"I wasn't," he said, and realized that was exactly what he was doing. Worrying about Raine.

She took a breath, as if ready to say good-night. But Alan wasn't ready to let her go. He bent down and touched his lips to hers. He felt her surprise, sensed her hesitation, and moved his mouth across hers, slowly, seeking a response. He tightened his grip on her shoulders to hold her in place, to keep her from moving away while he tasted her lips, felt the heat strike them both.

When Alan lifted his head, he looked down into a pair of very startled blue eyes.

"What the hell do you think you're doing?"

"Kissing you."

"For heaven's sake!" she sputtered as he released his hold on her shoulders. "Don't do that again."

"Why not?"

She glared at him. "You're practically a stranger."

"Wrong." He shook his head. "I'm the man sent to be your husband."

"Very funny."

"Oh?" His eyebrows rose. "That's what you told me just a few days ago."

"And you didn't believe me."

"And I still don't," he admitted. "But I've been thinking about kissing you all day. It was," he drawled, looking at her lips again, "very pleasant."

"Well, I'm glad you enjoyed yourself." She didn't sound glad. "Just don't do it again."

Of course, he didn't plan to. Alan let her step past him and leave the kitchen to return to her bed. He'd be out of here in a few weeks, as soon as some progress was made on the inheritance, as soon as he felt rested enough to return to work. He was supposed to be relaxing—not making passes at women in the middle of the night.

No matter how enjoyably.

RAINE WATCHED the social worker swing the state-owned station wagon into the street, Lily securely fastened into the car seat in the back. Charlie whimpered at Raine's feet, so she bent to pick him up and held him in her arms until the car was out of sight and the threat of tears had passed.

"Then there were five," Alan said behind her.

"Not for long, remember?" Raine sniffed and wiped her eyes before turning around. Charlie growled, so she told him to hush and put him down. He immediately went over to Alan and sniffed his feet.

"He isn't going to lift his leg, is he?"

"I hope not. I wasn't planning to wash floors today."

"I was more concerned with my slacks." Alan moved away from the dog, careful not to step on him. "Are you sure you're all right?"

She tried to smile. "Sure. I should be used to this. I just need to keep busy today, that's all."

"What are you going to do?"

"The kids are at day camp until three-thirty." She took a tissue from the pocket of her shorts and wiped her nose. "I thought I'd clean out the refrigerator and then go grocery shopping."

"I have a better idea."

Raine looked at him curiously. "Something from your list?"

"As a matter of fact, yes."

"Why am I not surprised?" She studied him, noting the color the sun had given him yesterday. He looked better, the lines in his face less prominent, the mouth more relaxed. The kiss last night had been more pleasant than Raine wanted to admit. It had been nice to stand in the darkness of her kitchen and enjoy the nearness of a man's body, his warm lips on hers. But nothing could change the fact that he was all wrong for her.

"I've realized I'm not the only one who could use a vacation," he said.

"Meaning me?"

"Yeah."

"That's really not your problem."

He shrugged. "I could tell Edwina that I thought my landlady was worn out. She'd probably tell Claire, and then..."

"Stop." Raine chuckled. "You're trying to threaten me, Alan. It won't work."

"No? You haven't heard what I had in mind."

"Okay, what?"

"Get that animal off my shoe and I'll tell you."

"Come here, Charlie," Raine ordered, motioning to the little dog. He hesitated at Raine's feet, then trotted into the living room, heading for his favorite chair. Raine turned back to Alan. "So?"

"The International Tennis Hall of Fame Championship starts today. We could go to La Forge for lunch— I haven't been there in years. Have you?"

She shook her head. "No."

"Then we could walk over to the tournament. Do you like tennis?"

"I don't get to many of the tournaments."

He looked at his watch. "We can leave in an hour, have an early lunch, then spend the afternoon watching some of the matches."

"I really can't—"

"Get ready in an hour? Sure you can."

"No, I have so much to do."

"Like what?"

"Groceries, cleaning, laundry..."

"I'll help."

"You?"

"Of course. Why not?"

"You're not exactly a domestic kind of guy."

"You don't know what kind of guy I am."

That was a challenge if she'd ever heard one. Raine smiled. "Maybe you're right." She looked into those cool, hazel eyes of his and grinned. "You've inviting me to lunch, tennis and offering to help with the groceries. What's the catch?"

"I'm bored."

"Right."

"No, really, I don't want to go by myself. Help me out."

Raine considered the invitation. It would be good to get out of the house and not think about missing Lily. She couldn't remember the last time she'd taken the day off and done something frivolous in the middle of the week. "You're serious about the grocery shopping?"

"Absolutely."

"Okay, you're on."

He looked as if he'd known all along that she'd agree.

SHADES OF ROSE PINK and forest green dominated the long porch of La Forge. Tucked beside the Tennis Hall of Fame, the restaurant had been sitting on Bellevue Avenue for over a hundred years. One of the staff led them down the steps to the wide porch. Trimmed in lattice, with cooling fans in the ceilings and wide windows overlooking the piazza, the room was a favorite dining spot for locals and tourists alike. Two young women, dressed in Victorian tennis dresses, lobbed tennis balls back and forth on the grass court outside the windows.

"I feel as if I've entered another century." Raine thanked the waitress who helped her into her chair and gestured at the window. "Can you believe it looks the same as it did when I was little?"

"Which was not a century ago," he said, smiling.

She ignored his teasing. "Claire used to bring my brother and me here at least once a summer, in the days when we summered here."

"With your father?"

She shook her head. "No. He never liked Newport," she said. "Said it was too crowded, too full of people who had too much time and too much money."

"Claire didn't agree?"

"No. Thank goodness, her philosophy of life was completely different."

A waiter interrupted to take their drink order, but when he left, Alan resumed the conversation. "And yet they were married."

"I never figured that out. My father had been a widower for years, the kind of man who kept to himself. I asked Claire once, before my father died, why she married him. 'He needed cheering up,' she said."

"From what I've seen, Claire is the kind of woman who can do just about anything she puts her mind to."

"Yes." Raine flipped open the heavy, plastic-covered menu. "Your being in Newport is living proof."

Alan looked blank, then comprehension dawned. He smiled, a slow, deliberate, charming smile that took Raine's breath away for a moment. "As the husband, of course."

"The last thing I need. Or want." Which wasn't quite true, but Alan didn't have to know that. She didn't want to hurt his feelings, after all.

"I'd think that with all those children, you'd need a man around."

"Why?" The suggestion hit a little close to home. She'd been trying not to worry, but watching Lily leave had been a sharp reminder of what was in store if she couldn't adopt Joey, Jimmy and Julie herself.

"What?"

"Why would I need a man around?"

He opened his mouth, then closed it again while he looked at her. He shook his head and tossed his menu to one side. "I give up."

"That was fast."

"It's not my usual way of handling problems."

She decided to return his teasing. "I meant the menu. You chose lunch quickly."

"You're doing this deliberately, right?"

"Right. You were getting too personal."

"We live together. *That*'s personal."

The waitress returned to deliver their drinks: iced tea for Raine and a Bloody Mary for Alan. "Would you like to order?" she asked.

Raine nodded. "I'll have the lobster roll plate."

"I will, too," Alan agreed, handing his menu to the waitress.

"We don't live together."

"I'm living with you and all those children. I'm sitting in the kitchen, I'm drinking iced tea on the porch, I'm swimming in the ocean, I'm—"

"For heaven's sake!" Raine interrupted, looking around at the other tables to see if anyone was listening to them. "Why are you getting so worked up over this? You should be pleased that you're not being considered husband material."

"Pleased is the understatement of the year."

"Then relax, or as Joey would say, 'Take a chill.'"

Alan removed his celery stick and took a deep swallow of the tomato juice while Raine sipped her tea and watched. She had to admire him—he wasn't shy about voicing his opinions. He was probably used to people being impressed with what he had to say and jumping to obey the orders he issued.

"What are you smiling about?"

"You're not used to being ordered around, are you?"

He grimaced, but his eyes crinkled at the corners in silent laughter. "No, sweetheart, I'm not."

"So, are you relaxing?"

"As much as I can."

"Good. That's an improvement."

"I'm working on it."

She leaned forward. Now seemed a good time to pry. "Why were you forced to take a vacation?"

"I collapsed at my desk." He winked. "Don't tell my mother."

"You collapsed? Why? What was wrong?"

"I told you before—overwork, exhaustion, high blood pressure, you name it—I had it."

"And on the stairs?"

"Exhaustion, I think. I talked to my doctor about that incident. You don't have to look at me as if I'm an invalid. There's nothing seriously wrong with me that a few weeks of fresh air and rest won't cure."

"I would have thought you'd want to be alone."

He shook his head. "I'd go crazy." The waitress set plates in front of them, and Alan thanked her. "I prefer people," he said. "And lobster for lunch."

Raine smiled at him. "You know, Alan, sometimes I like the way you think."

"Only sometimes?"

"Definitely only sometimes."

He picked up his fork and stabbed a thick chunk of lobster meat. "I can see I'm going to have to work harder to change your mind."

"You can try," Raine said, lifting a curly French fry. "In the meantime, thanks for the food."

THERE WAS A LOT to be said for spending an afternoon in the company of a handsome and charming man, watching other handsome and well-built men run around in shorts.

Tennis was so, well, *clean*. Despite the heat and the humidity, Raine was thrilled to be part of the crowd of spectators walking on the crunchy gravel paths behind the grass tennis courts. Alan filled in background information as she needed it, patiently answering all of her questions in a low voice. She'd forgotten how quiet the tennis matches were; the strict etiquette observed by the crowd assured the players of total concentration on their games.

The relentless heat from the sun made Raine glad she'd brought a wide-brimmed hat and worn a loose, cotton sundress. White was always a good choice for a Newport social occasion, Claire had stated more than once.

"If the heat's bothering you, we can use the box seats," Alan offered, watching Raine fan herself with her paper program.

"I'm fine," she said, pushing her sunglasses back up on her nose. The match was over, the Australian besting the young kid from Great Britain in two out of three. "I like standing here by the fence where I can see everything."

"If you change your mind, let me know." He looked at his program. "The best match of the day will be on the center court. We could go up on the bleachers and catch some of it."

He took her hand, surprising Raine with the easy gesture, and led her along a path beside a high green fence to the other side of the arena. Players warmed up on practice courts, while their coaches shouted encouragement and advice from the sidelines. Raine and Alan waited for the interval between sets to take seats in the bleachers.

"I can't believe it isn't crowded."

Alan shaded his eyes and watched the players. "It's the first day. By the end of the week, when the finals happen, this place will be sold out."

"Do you have tickets for the week?"

"My company does. If you want to come again, just say the word."

Raine smiled and looked down at the court as the next set began. She was having a wonderful time, but there was no reason to get carried away and plan to do it again. She watched the tennis players, she watched the crowd, she wiped her brow and discreetly fanned herself with the program. She promised herself she'd take up tennis again, even though it had been years since she'd held a racket. She wondered if she should give the children tennis lessons and how much they cost.

When the match ended, Alan stood up. "Let's go find the Del's lemonade cart."

"You're not going to pass out on me again, are you?"

He shook his head. "No. Despite meeting you in the kitchen last night, I managed to get a good night's sleep."

Raine wished he hadn't brought that up. It would have been easier to forget the way she'd responded to his kiss.

Alan didn't seem to notice her embarrassment. "What about you? Were you able to go back to sleep?"

"Sure," she lied. "No problem at all."

He took her hand to help her down the concrete stairs, then kept hold of it while they walked back along the path beside the fence. The green and yellow lemonade stand was three feet away when Raine stopped and attempted to tug her hand free.

"Alan!"

He didn't pay the least bit of attention and continued to hold her hand, even tighter, and smile at her as if she'd given him a secret signal. "Large okay?"

"Let go of my hand," she whispered, aware that there was a match going on nearby.

"What?" He bent down to listen to her. It was an intimate gesture, which made Raine even more nervous.

"Let go of my hand."

He looked surprised, but loosened his hold so she could pull away. "Better?"

"They're here."

"Who?"

Raine pointed to the two women bearing down upon them, parting the crowd like two ocean liners steaming up Narragansett Bay.

"Darling," one trilled.

"That's who," Raine said, feeling her heart sink. "The one called 'Darling' is Claire. The other one is your mother, right?"

"Yes," he managed to say. "Do you think they've seen us?"

"No jokes, please. Not now." She groaned. "They're going to eat us alive."

"We could make a run for—" But Alan was enveloped in a petite cloud of lavender cotton and gray curls before he could finish his sentence. Raine stepped back to avoid being run over, only to face Claire, slim and sporty in navy walking shorts and a white polo shirt.

Claire patted her stepdaughter's cheek. "Raine, you look a little warm."

"Well, I—"

"I'm so glad you could finally take some time away from the children. How are they?"

"Fine, Claire, but—"

"Isn't he something?" Claire lowered her voice. "And holding your hand, too. Fast worker, is he?" She winked. "I always loved a man who knew what he wanted."

"I don't think that's quite—"

"Never mind." Claire shook her head. "We'll talk later, in private. Wina is ready to catch up on all the news with her son, so we'll have the driver take us to your house." She turned to her friend. "Wina, we're going to Raine's now. Tell that handsome son of yours to lead you out of here before we totally succumb to the heat."

Wina hooked her arm through Alan's and smiled at Raine. "Raine, it's been so long. I can't wait to see Gertrude's house again and meet all of your children. You are so wonderful to let Alan stay at your place."

Raine managed a smile. "He's a perfectly lovely houseguest."

Claire arched one eyebrow. "Of course he is, darling. Didn't I tell you?"

6

"HOW DID YOU KNOW where to find us?"

Claire beamed, obviously quite pleased with herself. "I called your house, of course. You left a message on your answering machine."

Alan looked surprised. "You led them right to us."

"I can't leave the house without leaving a number, in case one of the children has an—"

"You look hot, dear," Claire said again, smoothing Raine's hair. "Are you feeling well?"

"Yes. Actually, now that I'm inside an air-conditioned limousine, I'm feeling quite cool." She crossed her legs and waved at Alan, who sat beside his mother. "Too bad you couldn't have hired something bigger."

Claire frowned. "Now, don't start with the sarcasm, Raine. You know I never learned how to drive."

"It's never too late," Wina interjected. She smiled at Raine. "I always tell her that, but she insists on hiring one of these big, silly automobiles."

Alan smiled at his mother, but steel threaded his voice. "You still haven't told me why you're here in Newport, Mother."

Edwina shot a plaintive look at Claire, then waved her tiny hands in the air as if to shoo away her son's questions.

Claire leaned forward and held out her hand. "Who is the best jeweler of all?"

"I have no idea," Alan replied. "And I have a feeling that it makes no difference whatsoever."

"Thames Street," Edwina finally sputtered.

Claire waggled her fingers. "I need to have this ring reset and there is no one else I'd trust."

Alan nodded politely in Claire's direction. "I'm sure that's true, of course," and the three women were aware he was sure of no such thing. "But," he continued, his tone even, "I wonder why you're not visiting with Alexandria and the children. Wasn't that part of your summer plans?"

"Later," his mother managed. "She's expecting us—me—later."

"After Claire sees the jeweler," Raine finished for her. She felt sorry for Edwina, who obviously hated to deceive anyone. And yet she and Claire had been friends for years. Who could tell what kind of schemes Claire had embroiled poor, flustered Wina in?

The limousine pulled to a stop in front of Raine's home, and the driver assisted the three women out of the car, then stood waiting for further instructions.

"Don't disappear," Alan told him. "They won't be staying long."

Raine watched the older ladies head toward the front porch and waited for Alan to step beside her. "Isn't that wishful thinking on your part?" she whispered.

"No, simply an accurate assessment of how long my patience will last."

"I warned you."

"Yes," Alan agreed, his eyes twinkling. "You certainly did." He took her arm. "Come on. We have to stick together through this."

Raine unlocked the front door and gave Edwina a brief tour of the downstairs as they headed for the kitchen. Lily's high chair still stood in its customary corner, so Raine quickly carried it into the utility room.

"This is lovely," Wina purred, her hands fluttering in the air again. "Simply lovely. I remember your great-aunt, of course, but I haven't been inside her home for years. Isn't it wonderful that she left it to someone who would love it the way she did?"

"Thank you." Raine set bright plastic pitchers of lemonade and iced tea on the kitchen table, while Alan retrieved clean glasses from the dishwasher and filled them with ice. It was a domestic scene, Raine noted, that would most likely send the ladies into raptures of delight. "Would you like to sit on the porch?"

Claire shook her head. "It's cool enough right here."

"Oh, I agree," Wina added, sitting down at the wide oak table. "Nice and cool."

Alan lifted a pitcher. "Who would like lemonade?"

"I would," Claire said. "With a touch of vodka."

"Me, too," Wina added.

Alan looked at Raine. "Above the sink," she said. "It's Claire's personal supply."

"Don't give me that look, Raine." Claire sniffed. "After that long trip, I could use a little sustenance."

"Long trip?" Wina asked.

"Of course it was long. Long and dry."

"Oh, yes."

Alan found the bottle and brought it to the table. "Where are you two staying? And for how long?"

Claire nodded approvingly at the generous amount of liquid he splashed into her glass. "I simply adore it when a man makes a drink."

"Maizie Chapman's cottage," Alan's mother answered. "Just for a little while."

Raine knew that the Chapman "cottage" was a thirty-room, oceanfront showplace. She sat down at the foot of the table and watched Alan hand Claire the drink, then make another for his mother. "I'll have tea, as long as you're playing host," she said. She looked at the clock over the refrigerator. "I have to go pick up the children at camp in fifteen minutes."

"Send the car," Claire replied airily.

"That's the vodka talking."

"No," Alan interjected. "Let the ladies make themselves useful."

"Well . . ." Raine hesitated. "Maybe this once."

"Write down the address."

"I'll need to go, too. They've been taught not to get into strange cars, no matter what."

Claire leaned toward Edwina. "Didn't I tell you what a lovely mother she'd make?"

"Oh, yes, yes." Wina was fluttering again. She turned to Raine. "How many children do you take care of, dear?"

"Five."

Claire frowned. "I thought there were six."

"The baby left today. But I'm expecting two more this week."

"Two more? My goodness."

"A brother and sister. They've been in a temporary placement, but they need—"

"That makes seven!" Claire gasped. "Are you going to hire a nanny?"

"I *am* the nanny, Claire. It's my job."

"You're much more than a nanny. You're—"

"Drink up, Claire," Alan ordered. "And I'll make you another."

"I'm going to need it," the older woman said, raising her glass to her lips. She took a long swallow, then smiled at her stepdaughter. "Life is certainly full of surprises, isn't it?"

LIFE WAS FULL of a lot of things, Alan decided later in the cool comfort of his third-floor room. And surprises were right up there at the top of the list. He was still in shock over last night. Not about kissing Raine, she'd looked sultry and sleepy in the middle of the night, and he had no regrets.

His reaction was the problem. Her lips packed one hell of a wallop. He didn't recall a simple kiss ever arousing him quite the way that one had. Maybe this enforced vacation was responsible for more than simple rest and relaxation.

Okay, he told himself. He hadn't had time before to enjoy kissing a woman in a dark kitchen, nor the satisfaction of holding her hand on a sunny summer afternoon. He'd missed feeling warm fingers in his palm and the sweep of a woman's hair against his shoulder. He'd like more—a whole lot more—but Raine tended to dance away whenever he got too close. She'd made it clear. All right, so he wasn't "perfectly lovely husband" material; being a husband was not a job he wanted.

But what in hell was the matter with him? He was an ordinary-looking guy who still had plenty of his own hair. There were a few wrinkles around the eyes, but he kind of liked them. He could be in better shape, but he'd been working on that. He still had all of his teeth and plenty of money. His secretaries liked him. His employees didn't use his face for a dart board.

But one tiny, dark-haired woman looked at him as if he were her worst nightmare come true.

Still, she'd let him kiss her. She'd even let him hold her hand. And she'd consented to lunch, too.

Maybe that crazy stepmother of hers was right, after all: life was full of surprises. He was certainly beginning to surprise himself.

RAINE WAS FOLDING LAUNDRY in the utility room when Alan found her. He leaned against the dryer and watched her fold a pile of towels into neat squares. "Good morning."

She smiled, ridiculously glad to see him. After yesterday, she felt as if they were friends, which made living with him a whole lot easier. "Good morning. You look like you slept well."

"I got up once—looked for you in the kitchen, but you weren't there. It was very disappointing."

Raine shook her head, refusing to be embarrassed by his teasing. "I never heard a sound. Yesterday wore me out."

"Where is everybody?"

"It's late. I already took them to camp." She stacked the towels on the table, pushed a couple of buttons to start the dryer and turned the dial on the washing machine. "Come on," she said, as the machines sprang into action. "I have to keep moving."

"You're always moving," he said, following her into the kitchen.

"I'm happy when I'm busy."

"You must be happy all the time, then."

She ignored the comment and pulled the plastic garbage can close to the refrigerator before opening the door.

Alan leaned against the counter. "I've been giving our problem some thought," he began, watching Raine frown at something in a plastic bag that she couldn't identify.

"You're talking about Claire and Edwina?"

"Right." At least he knew she was listening. "I think we should go along with them."

She tossed the bag into the garbage. "You've been out in the sun too long, Alan. Why don't you find a staircase and take a little nap?"

"Very funny." He reached past her and helped himself to a handful of green grapes.

"I'm not feeling funny. I'm trying to get ready for two new children *and* clean out this refrigerator so I have room for the groceries I need to buy *and* decide what to give everyone for dinner tonight *and*—"

"Everyone meaning the old ladies?"

"Yes. Remember how Claire invited herself?" She tossed a moldy cucumber into the trash. "I don't know why I buy those things. No one eats them."

"Tell me about the new kids. What usually happens?"

"You never know. Sometimes they're scared. Sometimes they're angry."

"What do you do?"

"Make them part of the family as quickly as possible. They'll take their cues from the other kids. With luck, they'll settle down." Raine certainly hoped so. There was enough turmoil in the house right now.

Alan finished the grapes and peered over Raine's shoulder. "What are you looking for now?"

"My yogurt."

"I don't see it." She winced. "I hope no one ate it."

He grabbed a can of soda. "I'll have cookies for breakfast instead."

"So much for health food." She removed a casserole dish and set it upon the counter, then tossed an empty ketchup bottle into the recycling bin.

"It has its drawbacks." He popped the top on the root beer and took a long swallow.

She frowned at the inside of the refrigerator again, then shut the door. "No plans today? No list?"

"I'm playing it by ear."

"That's unusual. Are you sure you're feeling all right?"

"No. And I won't be all right until Claire and Edwina have left the state."

"You shouldn't say that," Raine said, but smiled anyway. "It's not very nice."

"I say we beat them at their own game."

"How?"

"They want us together. So, let's be together."

"You don't mean in the biblical sense."

He most certainly did, but wouldn't admit it yet. "Sexually? No. Unless . . ." He grinned at her, putting a hopeful expression on his face.

"No, thanks. And quit teasing me while I'm trying to work."

"Okay. If we go along with their plans, they'll leave."

"Why would they leave? Wouldn't they hang around and gloat?" She sat down at the table and pulled a yellow legal pad and pen in front of her.

"No. They'd be off somewhere else. Two of my sisters are still single. They could go pick on them for change."

"So, mission accomplished, they'd fly off to the Hamptons to meddle in someone else's life."

"Exactly. You're right on top of things, Raine. I admire that in a woman."

"You don't have to be sarcastic. I'm trying to make a grocery list—and by the way, you owe me a trip to the supermarket, remember?"

Alan groaned. "I was hoping you didn't."

"No way, pal."

"Want to skip out of here and go back to the tennis tournament?"

"I thought you were going to give your tickets to your mother."

"I did, but I can always get more tickets."

"Aren't you going to spend time with her?"

"No. That's not part of the plan. Spending time with you is part of the plan."

Raine rested her chin on her hands and sighed. "I have this fantasy that someday I'm going to meet a single man, maybe one wearing one of those carpenter tool belts. He's going to want to go out with me just because he wants to, and not because it's part of somebody else's plan."

"Well, you can always dream, can't you?"

"I think it's easier not to."

"Uh-oh. Cynicism."

She shrugged and picked up her pen. "Call it what you want. I'm not sitting here waiting for Prince Charming to come along."

"Would you recognize him if he did?"

"That's a strange question."

"I'll tell you, honey, fairy godmothers could line up here in the street offering to grant your wishes and you know what?"

"What?"

"You'd tell them you didn't need anything." Alan stood up and pushed his chair in. "Let me know when you want to go grocery shopping. I'll drive."

Raine watched him leave, then doodled absently on her shopping list. What would she wish for, if she was sure it could come true? She thought for a long moment. She'd wish for a man to love, one who would love her in return. Someone strong and dependable and kind and sexy.

Alan Wetmore Hunter came close, especially in the strong and sexy categories, but she'd had a preview growing up of what it was like to live with a man who put business first. She wouldn't do that to her own children. She wanted her prince to go to school plays and coach Little League and pick up a gallon of milk at the store on his way home from work. She wanted him in bed with her at night, not working late at the office, especially if the office was on the other side of the world.

Raine picked up her pen and looked at the list in front of her. Enough daydreaming—it was back to reality. What on earth was she going to feed all these people?

TOBY AND CRYSTAL stood quietly beside the front door, identical expressions of fear in their big brown eyes. The social worker wished Raine luck and left, promising to be in touch at the end of the week.

Raine touched the little boy's shoulder. "Want to see the rest of the place?"

Toby stuck his lip out. "I don't like it here."

Raine knelt down so she could be at eye level with him. "You're eight, right?"

"Yeah."

"Wait till Joey and Jimmy come back from camp. They're your age, and they can show you around."

"I don't want to."

Raine turned to his younger sister, Crystal. "Would you like to see your room? You'll be sharing with Vanessa, but she's not home right now." The little girl nodded, then yawned. Raine noticed that her eyes were puffy; she looked as if she hadn't had any rest for quite a while. The social worker had said that the children had been abandoned a week ago and had stayed in a temporary shelter until a foster home could be found for them.

"'Kay."

The children stood next to two plastic garbage bags filled with their possessions, so Raine picked them up and led the youngsters to the front staircase. Alan came out of the living room, Charlie following at his heels.

The dog wagged his tail when he saw the children.

Toby frowned. "I don't like dogs."

"I do," his sister said, her eyes lighting up as the little furry animal tilted his head to look at her. "Is he a real dog?"

"Yes, he's real. Why does he like kids and not me?" Alan said, taking the bags out of Raine's hands.

"They say dogs sense things."

"What kind of things?" Toby said.

"I'm not sure, but I think dogs know things about people that we don't."

"I'm Alan," her houseguest offered, smiling at the newcomers. "I live upstairs."

The children didn't respond with anything other than petrified expressions, so Raine headed upstairs. Toby and Crystal hurried after her, with Alan following behind them. When they reached the wide hallway, Raine stopped at the first door.

"This is the bathroom," she said. "Anyone want to use it?" They shook their heads. "Okay, moving on." She stopped at the next open door. "Here, Toby." She pointed. "Joey and Jimmy have one set of bunk beds, and you can have the other. You can pick the top or the bottom."

"I don't like bunk beds."

"You're out of luck, then, because that's all there is," Raine stated cheerfully. "You get this dresser, too, so put your clothes away." She opened the closet and showed Toby the shelves full of puzzles, games and Lego sets.

"These belong to everyone," she explained. "Feel free to play with anything in here, just as long as you pick up your mess when you're done."

The boy looked a little less grumpy. "Yeah?"

"Private stuff is kept in boxes under the beds and no one else is allowed to touch." She took an empty box from the space under Toby's bunk bed and showed him. "See? You can put your special things in here and slide it right back under the bed so no one else will touch your stuff."

"Cool."

"What about me?" Crystal asked, tugging on Raine's pants. "Do I get a bed, too?"

"Of course you do, honey. Just follow me."

Alan caught Raine's eye and lifted his eyebrows. She shook her head and took Crystal's hand, leading the child across the hall to another bedroom, this one done in shades of yellow. Twin beds lined one wall, with a window in between. Opposite were two dressers, a dollhouse and the door to the closet.

"Which one is mine?"

"This one," Raine said, patting the yellow and white quilt on the bed on the right.

"It's so pretty."

"I'm glad you like it."

"I brought my Barbie dolls."

"Vanessa and Julie—that's another girl who lives here—like to play dolls, too. I'll bet you'll have lots of fun together." The child yawned again. "Why don't you crawl under the covers and take a little rest?" She picked up some books that lay piled on the floor and put them upon the bed. "Would you like to read?"

"Okay." The child kicked off her dilapidated sneakers and climbed into bed, gingerly stroking the pillow as if she'd never seen one before. She looked afraid to touch the books until Raine handed her one. "I'll be downstairs when you wake up."

"What about Toby?"

"He'll be with me," Raine promised. "You can meet the rest of the kids, too." Raine smoothed the dark hair from the child's face and stroked her brow as she snuggled under the sheet.

Alan stood in the doorway and watched the whole thing. It was amazing to him that children would not have beds or pillows or private places for their special toys. It was hard to believe that these children didn't have parents to take care of them, a roof over their heads or enough food to eat.

These kids had nothing except Raine and what she could give them.

Alan Wetmore Hunter III was impressed.

"COME ON. It'll be fun."

Raine tossed two heads of lettuce into the grocery cart. "You said that on Monday, and I ended up with Claire and Edwina drinking vodka in my kitchen."

"This will be different. Look, didn't you say they might be coming over to the house today?"

"Claire mentioned it, yes. But I'm not sure when."

He looked at his watch. "It's only ten. We'll be out of here in what—twenty minutes, tops?"

Raine looked at the pile of groceries in the cart. "Pretty close."

"Then we race home, put the food away and bail out."

"And go where? Someplace on your list?"

"As a matter of fact, yes. Touring a mansion or two is right up there at the top. I want to see how my ancestors tried to outspend each other."

Raine picked through the mushrooms and selected the freshest ones. "Which ancestors—the Wetmores or the Hunters?"

"Wetmores. One branch of the family owned Château sur Mer. My parents used to take us there years ago, but I've never seen any of the other mansions." He halted the cart when Raine stopped at the milk section. "How many?"

"Four," she said, trying to make room in the cart. "Then we're out of here."

"No ice cream?"

"It will be soft by the time we get home."

He opened the freezer door in front of the shelves of ice cream. "I'll risk it."

"What happened to yogurt?"

Alan tossed three half-gallon cartons of ice cream into the overflowing cart. "The boys and I are addicted to Heavenly Hash."

"I noticed. If you're going to sneak ice cream you'd better learn to rinse the bowls and put them in the dishwasher."

"Or buy paper."

"Good idea. How do you eat ice cream without the girls knowing about it?"

He shook his head. "I'm not telling. We made a secret pact."

Raine could believe it. In the last couple of days Alan had seemed more comfortable with the children, going out of his way to talk to them. Even grumpy little Toby, pleased to be included in Alan's secret ice-cream parties, had responded.

Just like me, Raine realized, *responding to the man's quiet charm despite my better judgment.* The children would take their cues from her, and so far no one had found any reason to avoid the houseguest. He'd relaxed into something almost human.

"We're going to have some fun," Alan stated, taking over the steering of the shopping cart. "I'm getting the hell out of here now. Then we're going for a tour of . . . what—The Breakers, Rosecliff, Marble House?"

"It's the busy season. There might be lines."

"I don't care. The kids won't be back until three-thirty, right?"

"Right."

"Then we have plenty of time." He started jogging toward the checkout stand. Raine hurried after him. He was difficult to argue with once he'd made up his mind.

She continued to hurry after him for the rest of the day. They put the groceries away in record time, with Alan looking at his watch while attempting to organize the placement of canned goods on the pantry shelves. She reheated leftovers in the microwave while he read the Newport guidebook aloud.

She accused him of being obsessive. He told her he was simply trying to bring some diversity into her existence. Raine didn't argue. Having a gorgeous man live in her house and direct her social activities was certainly different from her usual summers. She just had to remember that he'd be donning his business suit and flying off to the real world soon.

RAINE TRIED TO KEEP UP as they toured The Breakers, the Vanderbilts' summer mansion, with a large group of tourists eager to see an authentic home of the Gilded Age. Alan looked intrigued, seemed to absorb the information given by the tour guide, and asked several polite questions.

"Alice Claypoole Gwynne Vanderbilt. Any relation?" He stood in front of a large painting hanging above the second-floor landing.

"I doubt it," she whispered. "I think my father would have told me, but maybe not. He didn't talk much about himself."

"Maybe you should have inherited all of this," he teased.

She leaned closer. "Do you think it's too late?"

"It's never too late to go after what you want." Alan took her hand and tugged her toward their group, which was disappearing through a wide doorway. The guide allowed them a few minutes to admire the view of the green lawn and the ocean from the upper loggia before hustling the crowd through the rest of the huge mansion.

Raine was impressed most by the massive dining room. Red-damask-covered chairs lined the walls and surrounded a huge teak table.

"Above you, on the vaulted ceiling, is an oil painting of Aurora, Roman goddess of Dawn," the guide explained. "The Baccarat chandeliers were designed by Richard Morris Hunt and contain thousands of crystal beads."

Alan, several feet away on the opposite side of the table, winked at her. She knew he was thinking of her chaotic group at dinnertime. She couldn't quite picture anyone but royalty eating in this dining room. When the crowd moved toward the kitchen, Alan waited by the door.

"I keep losing you in the crowd," he said.

She was surprised that he said it as if he missed being with her. "Don't worry. I'm not sneaking off."

"Promise?" His grin was infectious.

"Promise."

"Can you get a sitter tonight?"

"Why?"

"How about an elegant seafood dinner somewhere, just the two of us?"

"Why?"

He frowned. "What do you mean—why?"

The guide gave them a pointed look and asked for quiet before describing the Vanderbilts' kitchen. After the tour, the group was led outside and invited to go downstairs to the basement souvenir shop.

"That was fun," Raine said, ignoring the signs for the gift shop. "Want to walk out on the front lawn?"

"Certainly," he said, taking her hand. "I don't want to miss anything."

They strolled across the wide expanse of grass toward the ocean, then headed through the high, cast-iron gates to Victoria Avenue. "Now, let's discuss dinner," Alan said.

"We can discuss it, but—"

"Didn't we agree to at least pretend to go along with the old ladies' plans for us?"

"Yes, but . . ."

"Then let's get them to baby-sit tonight while we go out for a romantic evening. They won't be able to refuse."

"A romantic evening will thrill them."

"What about you?" His voice was low.

"I've nothing against romantic evenings, but . . ."

"But not with me."

Raine didn't know how to deny the truth. "You're not my type." She looked sideways at his handsome profile. "No offense, and besides—I'm not your type, either."

"Really? And what exactly *is* my type?"

"That's easy," she replied. "Sophisticated. Elegant. The kind of woman who gives lavish parties without one single anxiety attack."

He looked uncomfortable, so Raine knew she'd been accurate in her description of the future Mrs. Wetmore

Hunter. He cleared his throat. "Do you know anyone like that?"

"Claire." Raine laughed as they turned off Bellevue Avenue and headed toward her home. "The perfect wife for a tycoon."

"Kiss me," Alan demanded, turning to take her into his arms.

"What?"

"Just do it," he whispered. "They're watching."

Alan's mouth closed over hers before she could utter a word of protest or assent. He urged her lips apart and deepened the kiss until Raine moaned. She didn't realize her arms had gone around his neck, or that her body had leaned into his until he lifted his head and the demanding pressure of his mouth on hers was gone.

"Thanks," Alan said, his eyes dark. A trace of a smile flickered across his mouth as he stared down at her. "That was almost as good as in the kitchen."

"*Who's* watching?" She slid her arms from around his neck and eased onto the soles of her feet. She'd been standing on tiptoe and hadn't even known it.

"Wina and Claire are waiting for us on the front porch."

"So?" For a banker, he sure could kiss.

"The plan, remember?"

"Oh, yes. The plan. Dinner."

"Smile at me and take my hand."

She did, wishing just for a second that there wasn't any plan—or, for that matter, that there were no matchmaking mothers or seven kids due home from camp. Raine took a deep breath and looked at the front porch. "Oh, no!" She raised her voice. "Don't open—"

In a flash Charlie swept past Claire's feet and out the screen door. He flew down the sidewalk and past Raine as she lunged to catch him.

"Charlie!" she called. "Come! *Come!*"

"What the hell—?"

"He runs away," Raine said, turning to race after the speeding little dog. "There are two female beagles down the street. I don't want him to get hit by a car!"

Raine shot down the sidewalk after the dog, cursing both him and her sandals. He hadn't run away in months, but she hadn't given him any opportunities, either. She'd fenced the backyard, so he was allowed to play outside with the children, as long as everyone understood that no gates were to be opened on any condition.

Alan caught up with her quickly. "I'll find him," he said.

"You don't know where he's going," she panted, her breathing labored.

"Tell me."

"Brown house, three stories, green mailbox with pineapples painted on the side."

"Got it. If I can't catch up with him, I'll grab him when I get there." Alan sped past her, and Raine slowed down, keeping her gaze on Charlie, who was running away from them as if it was all a game.

"Damn dog," she muttered. Who'd think a spoiled little lapdog would turn into a gazelle the minute he smelled freedom? She worried about him being hit by a car. After all, he was her best friend, the little ball of fur that slept on her feet in the winter and kept her toes warm. Raine kept jogging toward the brown house on the corner and watched Alan attempt to catch up with Charlie.

The next thing she knew, she landed facedown on the pavement.

7

ALAN THRUST the squirming bundle of fur into Raine's arms. "Take him before he bites. This idiot dog growled at me."

Charlie licked Raine's hand. "Bad dog," she scolded. "Only bad dogs run away."

"Come on," Alan said, reaching down with one hand. When Raine didn't take it, he frowned. "Why are you sitting on the sidewalk?"

"I'm not sure." Raine winced and tried once again to move to an upright position. "One minute I was running, the next thing I knew I was on the pavement. I think I may have twisted my foot or something."

"You're hurt?"

The concern in his voice amazed her. "I'm afraid I am. This is so embarrassing."

He knelt in front of her. "Which foot?"

"The right one." Alan touched her ankle with tentative fingers, then moved them lower, to the top of her foot where an ugly scrape oozed blood. "Ouch," she said. "There."

"I can't tell if anything's broken. Can you stand?"

"I think so."

"Well, hang on to that idiot animal while I help you up."

"Then what?"

"Either I carry you or we call an ambulance."

"I'm only one and a half blocks from home. I think I can hobble—ow!" She stood with his arm around her waist. Charlie whimpered and put his head upon her shoulder.

"Don't fight me, Raine. Just this once, don't fight me." Alan swept her up and into his arms, and Raine found herself tucked against his warm shirt. Charlie remained silent, which, Raine figured, showed a lot of sense. She decided to follow the dog's lead.

They rounded the corner to see Edwina and Claire waving goodbye to a large station wagon, the other half of the neighborhood car pool for day camp. The children stopped in the middle of the yard and stared at them for a moment before they broke into a noisy babble of questions.

"Oh, good," Claire called. "You caught him!"

Edwina hurried out of the yard. "Are you hurt, my dear?"

Vanessa started to cry. "Raine's hurt?"

"No," Raine called as they approached the gate. "Well, maybe a little, but I'll be okay."

Vanessa sniffed and joined the kids surrounding Raine asking questions.

"Somebody take the dog," Alan ordered, his voice rumbling above Raine's head. Jimmy rushed to obey him. "Everyone else out of the way so I can get Raine in the house." The children parted like the Red Sea.

Joey held the door open, the ladies fluttered behind them, and Alan carried Raine to her bedroom.

"No—the living room. The couch is fine."

He sighed and reversed direction. Once in the living room he set her gently upon the couch. "Don't move."

"I don't intend to, at least not yet."

"Oh, dear," Edwina moaned, wringing her tiny hands. "I had no idea the little dog would run out the door."

Claire patted her friend's shoulder. "Now, Wina. You mustn't blame yourself. Raine will be fine. Alan here will see to it."

Raine adjusted her leg so that her foot rested on the arm of the couch. "He will?"

Edwina sniffed. "He will?"

Alan frowned at all of them. "I will," he stated emphatically. "Would the two of you take the children into the kitchen and give them milk and cookies or something while I get some ice on this foot?"

"Here," Donetta said, standing nearby. She handed him the ice pack. When she saw his look of surprise, she added, "I got my first aid badge in Girl Scouts."

Alan nodded. "I believe you." He took the ice and held it on Raine's foot.

"I'm really fine," Raine insisted, wishing everyone would quit making such a fuss. She didn't like being the center of attention, especially since it had meant being cradled in Alan's arms for a block and a half. It had been altogether too irresistible, being held against that wide chest. She'd even rested her cheek against his shirt for the briefest of moments—until she'd realized what she was doing.

"How does that feel?"

"Very, very cold." She gritted her teeth, unwilling to admit that her foot was starting to hurt like hell.

Alan lifted the pack, and he and Donetta examined Raine's injury. "It's still swelling," he said. "Think we should get X rays?"

Donetta's eyes glowed. "Yes—just to be safe."

"I don't need—"

"Where's the hospital around here?"

Raine told him. "But I don't need to go there."

"You're a very cranky patient." He left the room, and Charlie hopped onto the couch next to Raine and snuggled against her.

"I'm not cranky, am I?" she crooned, petting Charlie's head.

"Yes, you are," Donetta said, perching on the couch across from Raine. "You're not cooperating."

"Okay, Doc." Raine smiled despite the shooting pains in her toes. "I promise to do better."

Alan returned to the room. "The mothers will watch the kids while I take you to the emergency room. We'll take the van. Where are the keys?"

"In my purse, but I don't think I need—"

"Don't move. I'll be right back."

He sounded as if he had it all figured out. Here was a man who liked to be in charge, and since he'd been on vacation he'd had no one to boss around. Until now. The man was in his glory, giving orders and expecting that they would be followed without question.

And there wasn't a darn thing she could do about it, except grit her teeth and pray.

"NICE BEDROOM." Alan looked around at the floor-to-ceiling bookcases and the tall windows in the octagon room. "I gather it used to be the library?"

"Go away."

"Can't," Alan said cheerfully. "I'm your nurse."

"This is a nightmare, right?" She threw one arm over her eyes as she lay on her bed, her foot in a thin, putty-colored cast and propped up on a pillow.

"Not exactly." He poked at a couple of the books that filled the shelves. "You have quite a collection."

"It's my hobby. Help yourself to anything you like."

Alan turned away from the shelves and sat down beside Raine on the wide bed. "Do you need one of the pain pills the doctor gave you?"

There was silence before she finally admitted, "Yes."

Alan opened the vial of pills on the nightstand and shook one into his palm. "Sit up a little," he said, waiting for her to lean back on her elbows before handing her the glass of water and the white capsule.

"Thanks," she murmured, then took the medicine. She handed the glass back to him and her smile was rueful. "I hate being dependent on anyone."

"I noticed."

"It's just that I don't know what I'm going to do, cooped up in this room with seven kids...."

"I'll take care of everything."

She pressed her lips together. "It hurts when I laugh."

"Really," Alan insisted, hearing himself say the words but not believing them. "I can handle everything around here. The doctor said nothing was broken, the ligaments are torn and are going to be painful for a while, but—"

"But I'm in a cast."

"A soft one."

"Still . . ."

"You have me and two grandmothers available, too."

Raine rolled her eyes. "I hope your mother is more maternal than mine. Where is everybody?"

"Out to dinner," Alan confessed. "Claire put everyone in the limo and headed to her club."

Raine groaned. "Why couldn't she have just gone to McDonald's or called out for pizza?"

"I don't think that's the way her mind works."

"Were they clean?"

He knew she was talking about the kids and not their respective parents. "I don't know. They were gone when we got back. My mother left a note."

"I feel rotten," Raine confessed. "And stupid."

"Speaking of stupid, here comes Charlie."

He hopped onto the bed, shot Alan a disgusted look, turned his back on him and curled up by Raine's knees. Alan envied the dog his position. He wouldn't mind curling up anywhere against Raine's delectable little body. Kissing her was just the beginning.

"What can I do to make you feel better?"

He knew she wanted to say "Go away" again, and wished he hadn't given her such an obvious opening to get rid of him. This was a rare moment. After all, they were alone. In bed.

The scene had its charms.

"Could I have a washcloth?" She pointed to a door on one side of the room. "There's a bathroom in there. I'd really like to wash my face."

When he returned with the cloth she reached for it, but he didn't give it to her. "Let me," he said.

"Alan," she began, but he didn't wait for her protest. Instead he took the warm, damp cloth and passed it lightly over her forehead, moving back her bangs as he did so. He traced the lines of each eyebrow, while Raine closed her eyes and sighed.

"Okay?"

"Mmm," she murmured.

He needed no further encouragement, and gently wiped her face with soft strokes of the cloth until he reached her lips.

The temptation was too great. Alan lowered his head and touched Raine's lips with his own, the forgotten cloth still gripped in his hand. He felt the gentle pressure of her fingertips across the nape of his neck, then her lips parted. He tasted the sweet warmth there, and he heard the little moan in the back of her throat, an entrancing sound that made him long to stretch beside her on the bed and take her right there.

But making love to an injured woman who couldn't get away was not exactly a noble idea, no matter how willing the lady appeared.

Alan lifted his head and looked down—into the surprised expression in Raine's blue eyes. Surprised, but not angry, he was glad to see. There was hope, after all.

"Do it again," she murmured, her lips turning up at the corners. Her hands slipped to his shoulders.

It was the last thing he'd expected to hear. "Why?"

"It makes my foot stop hurting."

"Well, that's a good enough reason," he answered, bending over her again as she twined her fingers around his neck.

This time he couldn't be gentle. This time he needed to explore the tantalizing textures of her mouth, feel the warmth of her lips parted only for him. Raine sank back against the mound of pillows and Alan followed, his chest touching her breasts, his hands braced at her sides. He felt her fingers glide through his hair, and her touch made him long to lie beside her and continue making love to her until they were both naked and sated.

He lifted his lips from hers when he heard the excited chatter at the front door. Raine opened her eyes and smiled at him. "Thanks," she murmured, her voice sleepy.

"Thanks?" No woman had ever thanked him for kissing her until now. *"Thanks?"*

"Mmm," she said. "For the pill and the kisses. I'm feeling better."

Claire poked her head into the bedroom. "We're back," she informed them unnecessarily.

Alan shot Raine a look filled with regret and slid off the bed.

Claire tiptoed into the room. "How's your foot, dear?"

"Feeling much better, Claire. There's nothing broken."

"But isn't that a cast?"

"Torn ligaments," Alan supplied. "More painful."

Raine looked at her leg. "'Fraid so. I'm supposed to stay off of it for two weeks or until it doesn't hurt."

"But however will you manage—"

"I'll call the social worker in the morning. Maybe I can arrange something."

"You won't need to," Claire stated. "I'm here to help."

"You are?"

"Well," Claire said, twisting her rings, "of course."

Edwina knocked on the open door. "There are some worried people who need to see that you're all right."

Raine waved at her. "Bring them in."

The seven children surrounded the bed, their eyes wide at seeing Raine lying there.

"Does it hurt?" Julie wanted to know.

"A little."

"Do we have to go away?" Donetta asked, examining the cast carefully without touching anything.

"Why would you think that, honey?"

Donetta shrugged. "It's happened before."

Vanessa's eyes filled up with tears, and Raine pulled her close to her. "No one is going anywhere. Grandma Claire is going to help."

"And Auntie Edwina, too?"

"Yes, Nessa. I'm sure she will." Raine looked past the children surrounding the bed, but Edwina and Claire had left the room. Alan still remained beside the bed, his hand close to the headboard. "Tell me about dinner," she said to the children. "Where did you go and what did you have to eat?"

Toby edged close to the bed. "We rode in a *limousine*," he whispered, as if confiding a secret. Crystal nodded, her dark eyes huge.

Joey added, "It was so cool."

"Totally awesome," his twin agreed.

Julie edged close to the bed and Raine put her arm around the child. "What did you have to eat? Hamburgers? French fries?"

The little girl shook her head. "Lobster," she informed Raine.

"*Lobster?*"

Donetta nodded. "To 'broaden our horizons.'"

Alan made a strangled sound, then covered it with a cough.

"I'm almost afraid to ask what you had for dessert," Raine finally said.

Joey shrugged. "Anything we wanted."

"From a—" Julie stopped and wrinkled her brow.

"Cart," Jimmy supplied. "We picked what we liked and the guy came back and gave it to us."

"And you all said 'Please,' and 'Thank you,' I'm sure."

All seven heads bobbed up and down.

Alan stepped forward. "Okay, everyone. Time for Raine to rest, so go play or whatever you do after dinner. . . ."

"They take showers," Raine told him as the children gave her kisses and hugs. "And play outside in the backyard—before the showers, that is."

"Bedtime?"

"Seven-thirty for the little girls, eight-thirty for the boys, and nine for Donetta, but everyone can read in bed."

"I'll be right out," Alan told them. He sat back on the bed and faced Raine. "How's your foot?"

"Better." She yawned. "I'll be running around here in no time at all. But Alan, I don't think Claire and Edwina are up to taking care of this crowd."

"What about me?"

She shook her head. "It's a big job for a paying guest."

"It will help me get back in shape for the real world." He kissed her lightly on the lips before sliding off the mattress. "Call me if you need anything."

"Thanks." She watched as he left the room and closed the door quietly behind him. From a mansion to the emergency room, it had been quite a day. She hadn't expected Alan would take care of her, hadn't known that his arms would feel so good when he carried her back and forth from the car to the hospital and home again.

It had been a heady sensation, having this man all to herself for a change. His lips had felt wonderful against hers, warm and demanding. She didn't want to think about how different they were, or who he was or, or anything important at all. She'd felt safe from the minute he'd lifted her from the sidewalk and swung her into his arms.

He'd be returning to his "real world," but it was tempting not to think about that particular departure. Alan Wetmore Hunter might prove to be Prince Charming, after all. A Prince Charming with an office half a world away.

"THIS IS GOING VERY well," Claire declared.

"It is?" Edwina followed her out of the kitchen and into the small bathroom.

"Of course. Shut the door." Edwina did, and turned to face her friend. Claire looked at herself in the mirror and smoothed several gray hairs into place. "I'm so smart."

"Yes, Claire, you are, but . . ."

"All we have to do now is get out of the way."

"I thought we were going to stay and help. We promised, didn't we? And the children are so much fun. Did you see Jimmy's face when he saw the chocolate cake?"

"That was Joey, Wina. Jimmy took the raspberry torte. Did you see Vanessa? She buttered both sides of her bread." Claire turned away from the mirror and put her hands upon her hips. "We are going to *pretend* to help Alan, of course. But we're only going to get in the way."

"Oh," Edwina said, frowning. Then comprehension dawned. "He'll have to do everything all by himself, including taking care of your lovely stepdaughter!"

"Your future daughter-in-law," Claire corrected with a wink.

"I can hardly wait. Do you think they'll have one of those long engagements?"

Claire shrugged. "You tell me—he's your son. Does he take a long time to make up his mind about things like this?"

"I don't know. I don't think he's been in love for years. But he usually goes after what he wants, once he's decided what he wants. Just like his father, bless him."

"Did you see the looks on their faces when we walked in? They'd been kissing—I'd bet my diamonds on it."

"I know," Wina said with a sigh. "She looked a little stunned, didn't she?"

"Surprises are good for Raine," her stepmother declared. "Especially passionate ones. She's much too set in her ways."

"Unlike us." The future mother-in-law reached for the doorknob. "Two mature women who have experienced our share of passion."

"Edwina! You make us sound positively exciting!"

RAINE LEANED ON Aunt Gertrude's old oak cane and limped toward the kitchen. Spending yesterday in her bedroom had almost driven her crazy. Despite the frequent rests on the couch, she'd always felt as though she was missing out on everything. It wasn't easy being bossed by three people—three people who didn't have a clue how a household with a lot of children operated.

They expected her to sit in bed and read magazines and drink iced tea as if she had nothing better to do, for heaven's sake.

Thank goodness they asked a lot of questions. She could answer questions. She *liked* answering questions. She would, if she wanted to, sit in the kitchen and answer questions all day long. She heard the familiar tones of Alan's voice and peeked through the doorway.

"No," Alan insisted. "Absolutely not. In fact, I think the two of you need some time off."

"Time off?"

"You're going to wear yourselves out," he declared, slapping peanut butter onto a slice of bread. He picked up another slice of bread and repeated the motion.

"Well . . ." Claire hesitated. "If you insist."

"I do." He turned to the women; each held a little girl on her lap. "Grape or strawberry?"

"Grape," they answered in unison.

Edwina sighed. "Maybe we'll head up to Alexandria's for a few days. What do you think, Claire?"

"If Raine doesn't need me, I suppose I could go with you."

"Go. Have fun. I don't need you," Raine said from the doorway. She smiled at her stepmother to soften her words. "Really."

"Darling," Claire called. "What are you doing out of bed?"

"My foot doesn't hurt," she fibbed. "I thought I could help out here."

Alan finished putting sandwiches in wax paper bags. "Everything is under control."

"I see that," she murmured, strangely unsettled. He looked so strong and handsome, standing there in his black bathing trunks and white T-shirt. "What are you doing?"

"Fixing lunch for the gang."

"Where is everybody?"

"Upstairs getting dressed, I hope." He glanced at the clock. "They have to leave in fifteen minutes, right?"

Raine nodded and hopped over to take a seat at the table. She couldn't believe Alan had made lunch for the kids.

"I got the dirt out," Donetta said, entering the room with the cooler in her arms. "Hi, Raine! Are you feeling better?"

"Why are you wearing a dress?"

Donetta shrugged. "Everything else is dirty."

Raine's heart sank. She'd forgotten about the laundry.

Claire noted the expression on Raine's face and quickly spoke. "I'll take her shopping after camp."

"Uh, that's not quite the solution, Claire." Raine started to get up from her chair. She grabbed the cane and lifted herself to her feet. "I'll just go throw a few things in the washing machine."

"It's under control," Alan said. "You're supposed to stay off your feet."

"But . . ."

"The doctor said."

"When did you get so bossy?"

"I learned from you." He put his hands upon her shoulders. "Go on. We're doing just fine."

Alan watched her limp off, every muscle in her body shouting reluctance at having to walk away from the running of her household and her seven little charges.

Doing just fine? Now *that* was a joke. He'd spent hour after hour trying to keep kids fed and clean. He hadn't had time to answer several important calls from New York or examine contracts expressed from Frankfurt. Claire and Edwina were practically worthless, complicating the simplest chore with advice and endless details to discuss. If they just left, he'd be better off.

This fatherhood business was enough to drive a man crazy.

"Phone, Alan!" his mother called.

He gave Raine's backside in those cute yellow shorts one last, longing glance before turning back to the kitchen. He took the receiver from Edwina as Vanessa walked past him, her hand in a box of cereal. Donetta was putting nail polish onto her fingertips, and the boys were nowhere to be seen. "Could you make sure they're all ready for camp?"

"Of course, darling." She motioned to Donetta to put the polish away and follow her.

Alan sighed and turned towards the wall. "Hello?"

"Mr. Hunter? This is Atwater, Brenner and Horton calling. Can you hold for Mr. Atwater?"

The Benjamin Atwater who could help him with the will? Alan couldn't believe he'd forgotten about that problem for a few days. "Gladly."

Within seconds, a man's voice boomed through the receiver. "Mr. Hunter, I understand you're unhappy with your grandfather's will."

"That's an understatement. I've come to Newport to see what could be done to speed up this inheritance."

"You're not close to marriage, I hear."

"No." Somehow Alan didn't sound as emphatic as he'd hoped. A vision of Raine leaning against the bed pillows flashed in front of his eyes. He quickly banished the idea. Marriage was not the solution, especially to Raine. He'd be required to make peanut butter sandwiches for the rest of his life.

"That *is* the easy solution, but if it's not an option, then we'll have to consider the alternatives. Your lawyers have been in touch with us in the past six months, but your grandfather's will is very clear."

"There's no other way?"

"The property still reverts to the state if there is no married grandson to inherit."

"I was afraid you'd say that."

"You can challenge the will and tie up everything in court for years, though. I'm sure you know that."

"I had hoped it wouldn't come to that."

"So did I. I enjoyed your grandfather. He was quite a character." There was a brief pause. "Proceedings will begin August 19, the twenty-fifth anniversary of his death. I'll look forward to meeting you, Alan. Come by the office any Tuesday and I'd be happy to discuss this with you."

Alan thanked the man and hung up the phone. There didn't seem to be anything else he could do about the will, except leave it to the lawyers to settle. Right now he had more immediate problems. He leaned against the counter, his hip soaking up a puddle of milk, and surveyed the disaster before him. The sink was full of cereal bowls, the table covered with boxes of cereal, spoons and bits of frosted cornflakes.

So much for his plan to make love to Raine. He'd been so consumed with kids and food and everything else in this crazy house, he hadn't had time to devote himself to the very intriguing woman who liked his kisses.

Well, Alan decided, picking up a sponge. It was time to make some changes around here.

8

RAINE FELL ASLEEP watching "Regis and Kathie Lee" interview a pet psychologist on their morning talk show. When she awoke, the familiar ache in her foot had subsided. The fan blew air gently across the bed, and the lace curtains moved slightly in the Atlantic breeze. She picked up the remote control and flicked the television off, then listened to footsteps in the hall.

"Alan?"

The door opened slowly. "Raine? You're awake?"

"Come on in."

Alan stepped inside and smiled as he crossed the room to the bed and sat down next to her. "How are you doing?"

"Much, much better."

"Is that the truth?"

She nodded. "Cross my heart."

"Want some lunch?"

Raine hadn't felt hungry until he mentioned lunch. "Yes, but you don't have to wait on me. I can come to the kitchen."

"Don't move," he ordered, sliding off the bed. "I'll be right back."

Raine hobbled to the bathroom and washed her face. She looked at her pale face in the mirror, quickly brushed some blush onto her cheeks and combed her hair. She climbed back into bed, wishing Alan would come back and kiss her again, the way he had yesterday.

Raine mentally shook herself. She was in danger of falling in love with this man, and she'd better watch out. He was charming and sexy and kind—qualities she'd given up hoping to find in a man, especially one with designer suits and an international life-style. But he spent too much time with his computer, and openly admitted he put business before pleasure, even at the expense of his health.

Alan didn't look like a banker when he returned in less than ten minutes, carrying a tray filled with sandwiches, two glasses of iced tea and a bowl of fruit salad. His T-shirt was stained with strawberry jam and Charlie trotted behind him.

"I can't believe this," she said, as Alan placed the wicker tray over her lap. Charlie hopped onto the bed and snuggled against her knees.

"Enjoy." Alan sat down facing her. His thigh brushed her legs, which, Raine decided, added an extra pleasure to the lunch in front of her. He picked up one of the glasses. "Mindy called. She's the social worker I met last week?"

"Yes. For the twins and Julie."

"She said to tell you she hopes you're feeling better, and if you need anything, just let her know and she'll see what she can do. She said she'd call when she gets back from her vacation."

"Okay. Anything else?"

"Your neighbor brought over a chocolate cake and thanked Claire for letting her kids ride in the limousine. And someone named Janet Damon called."

"She's Lily's new mother. Is anything wrong? What did she say?"

"She said to tell you that Lily is doing fine. She left her phone number."

"That was really nice of her." She always felt better if she knew that "her" children were doing well in their new homes.

"Eat up," Alan suggested. "And I'll tell you where our mothers are."

"Where? Out shopping for designer children's clothes and picking out lobster for dinner?"

He grinned at her and raised his glass in a mock toast. "I convinced them to take some time off. They've gone to Long Island to visit my sister."

"That should calm things down around here, but it leaves you with all the work," Raine protested.

"Don't worry about it. They haven't been much help, anyway. You'd never know my mother had raised five children."

"Tomorrow's Saturday. I should be able to be up and around all weekend. I need to get to the bank. You must have had to put gas in the van, and I want you to keep track of everything, so I can pay you back. The kids usually do as they're told, even Toby and Crystal. It's the grocery shopping that's the major problem. And the driving—"

"Raine," he interrupted. "Enjoy your lunch. I've taken care of everything."

She frowned at him, but picked up a fork and speared a melon ball. "You keep saying that."

"Well, you don't have to do everything. I have it all figured it."

"You do?"

"Of course. I've given it a lot of thought."

She picked up half of a sandwich and looked to see what kind it was. "Bacon, lettuce and tomato. Very nice."

"Claire told me you liked BLTs."

Raine put down the sandwich. "Why are you doing all of this?" Alan shrugged and looked uncomfortable, but Raine held his gaze. "You should be at some fancy hotel, and we both know it."

He glared at her. "That's the trouble, sweetheart. You think you know everything about me, just because you labeled me the first afternoon we met. Yes, I admit to working long hours and making a great deal of money, and I'm not going to apologize for it. I earn every dollar. And yes," he continued, leaning closer to her, "I desperately needed a vacation, and I'm fortunate to be able to take the time off and stay in this old house with a very beautiful and desirable black-haired woman who doesn't have the sense—"

"That's not true. I have plenty of sense."

"—to realize how attracted I am to her."

"You are?"

"Constantly." He stood up and took the tray off Raine's lap, then set it upon the floor. Then he reached over her and lifted Charlie.

"What are you doing?"

"Creating some privacy," he muttered, walking to the door and putting the little dog out. He shut the bedroom door, oblivious to Charlie's whimpers of complaint. "Pretty soon seven children are going to be traipsing into this room to tell you all about their day. I want you first."

"That's really not—"

"Where were we a few days ago?" He sat down on the bed and faced her once again. "I think we were kissing, don't you?"

"Do you realize how much you interrupt me?"

"Do I?"

"Yes," she whispered as he leaned closer. "It drives me nuts."

"Good," he said, touching her lips lightly with his. "Then we're even."

Raine hadn't the faintest idea what the man was talking about, especially after his lips captured hers once again and all thoughts left whatever brain she had left. It was natural to lift her hands to his shoulders, natural to respond to the pressure of his lips. His mouth was insistent upon hers, his tongue teased her lips. Raine felt herself transformed into lazy heat, unwilling and unable to move. Heaven, she decided, was kissing Alan Hunter. Raine wished she could go on kissing him for the rest of the hot July afternoon.

His lips finally released hers, but only to skim along her jawline, nibble one earlobe and move down her neck, which suddenly turned into tingling warmth as his lips trailed a path to her breastbone, visible in the open neckline of her shirt.

This was crazy, Raine thought, but she didn't want to think about common sense or reality; she simply yearned to feel this man's touch. Alan's fingers slid underneath her shirt and caressed her skin, sending ripples of pleasure throughout her body. His hand cupped one lace-covered breast in his palm.

He lifted his head and looked into her eyes. "You have a gorgeous body."

"You told me that once before."

"I did?"

"Yes. The second day you were here. You said I wasn't your type."

"I don't remember. I guess I changed my mind." His thumb teased the nipple through the lace, sending warmth streaking through her body now, settling in a very specific place. "You're very much my type, after all."

Raine touched his face, running her palm along his cheek and touching his upper lip with one finger. "Which is?"

"Smart."

"But you must have known a lot of intelligent women in England."

He looked thoughtful, then added, "None as funny as you are."

"Funny like ha-ha or funny-weird?"

He thought for a minute. "Both."

"Oh."

"And loving."

"You don't know that."

Alan shrugged as if her observation didn't affect him. "And sexy."

"You don't know that, either."

"Sweetheart, I can tell."

"How?"

"A man just knows."

She didn't really believe him. "And are you my type?"

"I doubt it, sweetheart." He sighed and withdrew his hand, leaving Raine with a sense of loss. Then he grinned at her. "Unless you'd prefer designer clothes and penthouses in three cities to grocery shopping in Newport?"

She knew then that he was kidding. "You'll have to keep looking for someone like Claire."

Alan grimaced and moved off the bed. "Please, don't mention that name," he said, then walked out of the bedroom, smiling as he shut the door behind him.

She wasn't his type. He wasn't hers. Raine told herself that it was for the best, that being caressed by this man could only lead to heartache and pain.

She wasn't willing to welcome either one into her life.

"OKAY, EVERYONE. Pick up your own mess."

This Saturday evening there was a lot of mess to pick up, Raine decided, looking around the living room from her position on the couch. The children had talked Alan into letting them eat hot dogs on the front porch, but the mosquitoes had driven them inside, where the little girls had insisted they eat in the living room.

"A real picnic," Vanessa had whispered. Raine had watched Alan melt as he'd looked into the child's big dark eyes.

Now the oriental carpet was littered with potato chip crumbs and even a few blobs of dried ketchup, but Joey appeared in the doorway with the vacuum cleaner.

Raine looked at him in amazement. "Do you know how to work that?"

Joey grinned. "No problem. Alan told me to just plug it in and start moving it around."

Crystal curled up beside Raine on the couch and yawned.

"Sleepy, honey?"

The child nodded and Raine put her arm around her. Raine wished she could take her up to bed, but for now they had to be content to snuggle together on the couch.

The noise from the kitchen was incredible. "WRX Classic Rock and Roll" blasted from the radio. The vacuum cleaner roared to life and Charlie hurried out of the living room, presumably to take refuge on Raine's bed until the noise died down. Alan entered the room, a dish towel tied around his waist, protecting his obviously designer jeans from ketchup and mustard.

"We're eating in the kitchen from now on," he stated, wielding a sponge against a ketchup splatter. "You should have warned me."

"I did," Raine said, trying to stop herself laughing. Alan conquered the stain, then sat down on the couch and stretched his long legs in front of him. He watched Joey turn off the vacuum cleaner and carry the machine out of the room.

"Great job, Joe!"

The boy grinned. "Thanks."

Raine yawned. "Who's doing dishes?"

"Nobody."

Raine had visions of mounds of dirty plates littering the counters. She wondered if she wanted to go into the kitchen and see for herself. "Nobody?" she squeaked.

"We don't wash. We throw them out. I bought a couple of cases of paper plates, cups, plastic silverware, things like that."

"A couple of *cases*? I'm only going to have this cast on for another ten days."

"It makes life easier."

A typically male solution to a problem. But a solution, nonetheless. She bit her tongue and decided to change the subject. She looked at Crystal. "Time for bed, honey. Would you tell Donetta that I need her help getting you ready?"

Crystal's eyes filled with tears. "My mommy went away. I don't know where she went."

"You must miss her." Raine stroked Claire's hair and met Alan's shocked gaze over the child's head.

"Sometimes—" the child thought for a minute "—sometimes Toby gets mad."

"At you?"

"Uh-huh."

"I know," Raine said, choosing her words carefully. "But I think Toby gets mad at everybody. I think he has a lot of 'mad' inside."

"He likes it here."

"You think so?"

"Yup. He told me to be real good and not wet my bed anymore so we could stay."

"You can stay, even if you wet the bed."

"Really?"

"Really. Now go get Donetta for me, okay?" The little girl jumped off the couch and ran through the dining room to the kitchen.

"Do they always come out with things like that?"

"Yes. You never know when they're thinking about their families or worrying about what's going to happen to them next."

"I never thought of it that way," he said. "And I've never asked you much about why these kids are here." Alan lowered his voice. "I guess I figured the kids didn't know their parents and didn't care."

"Oh, they care all right. Very much."

"I see that." He moved over and put his arm around Raine's shoulders. "What about Crystal's mother? Do you know where she is?"

"No. I don't think anyone does. She left the kids alone in an abandoned car. One of the neighbors noticed and called the police."

Alan swore softly under his breath. "At least they're safe now."

Raine leaned back against his arm, grateful to have his strength beside her, warm and solid. "That's the whole idea."

One of the boys screamed from the kitchen. "Sounds like a food fight to me," Alan muttered, leaving the couch. "Guess I'll go kick some butt."

It really was remarkable that a stranger could take over her house, with her children and everything else involved. All day Raine had paid close attention to the children's behavior and had not noticed that they were nervous or upset by the changes in the house. Maybe there was a lot more to Alan than she had given him credit for.

RAINE LEANED against the sink and eyed the ancient, claw-footed bathtub with longing. Claire had helped her with a sponge bath, but that had been less than satisfying. Raine longed to soak in the deep tub, preferably for two or three hours, and read the historical romance she'd bought six months ago and hadn't had time to open.

If she could step into it with her good foot, she could hang the right one over the edge of the tub, keeping the cast safe and dry.

It was worth a try, she figured. She'd kissed all of the children good-night. Alan, in some strange imitation of boarding school, had made sure everyone was in bed with their lights out. No one had griped too much, except Toby, and no one knew what he would do if he couldn't gripe.

Alan hadn't come downstairs again, so Raine assumed he had gone up to the peace and quiet of the third floor and would remain there until morning.

So, it was just her and the tub. Raine leaned over and turned on the faucets, then found the bottle of foaming bath oil Claire had given her for Christmas. After squirting some into the water, the scent of apple blossoms filled the black-and-white-tiled bathroom. Raine retrieved her book from the nightstand and stripped off her clothes before limping back into the bathroom. She tested the water, added more hot water and carefully eased herself in.

It was heaven on earth, she decided, drying her hands on a towel. Her foot was propped out of harm's way and her body luxuriated in the silky water. She reached for her book and opened it to the first page, ready to enjoy every minute of steamy silence.

An hour and a half later, Raine yawned and tossed the book onto the tiled floor. The water had cooled and her leg had grown stiff. She couldn't wait to curl up in bed and continue with the story of love in Montana. Unfortunately she couldn't figure out how she was going to get out of the tub.

"Raine? I just thought I'd say good night," Alan said from the hallway.

"Oh, okay. Good night."

"Are you okay?"

"I'm in the tub, that's all."

She heard the bedroom door open and his footsteps cross the room to the bathroom door. "In the tub? How'd you do that?"

"It's kind of hard to explain, but I'm fine. In fact, I'm ready to get out." To prove her intentions, she nudged the stopper with her toes until it popped out of the drain, releasing the water.

There was silence. "I'll wait here to make sure you can manage."

"I can manage," she insisted, but looked at her outstretched leg and naked body and tried not to laugh out loud. She wasn't sure she could get herself out of this, after all, though all she had to do was turn around, so that her good leg was on the outside of the tub and she could swing it onto the floor.

"Raine?"

"What?"

"Why is everything so quiet?"

"I was thinking."

"You can't get out of there, can you?"

The last of the bathwater gurgled down the drain. "Of course I can. I'm planning the best way, that's all."

She heard an impatient male sigh, then Alan's voice. "That's it. I'm coming in."

"What? You can't!"

"Sure I can. Can you reach a towel?"

"Yes, but—"

"Then cover yourself with it, because I'm not going to let anything happen to you."

"Nothing's going to happen to me," Raine grumbled, but reached for the towel, just in case he meant what he said. She dried herself as best she could, then wrapped the towel around her body, carefully covering herself in pink terry cloth.

The door opened a couple of inches. "All set?"

"Yes." Raine began to think this whole bath idea had been crazy.

Alan stepped inside, walked over to the tub and frowned at her. "How did you think you were ever going to get out of there?"

"I had it planned," she said, relieved that the towel covered so much of her. "I was going to turn around so that my good leg was on the outside." She made a face and looked back at her foot. "I thought that would be easy, but I'm not sure where to start. I didn't count on stiff muscles."

"Obviously." He put his hands onto his hips. He'd obviously showered, because his dark hair was damp on the ends and his short-sleeved, button-down shirt looked crisp and fresh.

"Are you going out? You're all dressed up."

He put his hands into the pockets of his linen slacks. "I was going to the movies."

Raine felt a stab of jealousy. Did he have a date? "Sounds fun. Don't let me make you late."

"You won't." But he didn't sound convinced; he stepped closer and peered at her.

"Don't step on my book."

Alan looked down and picked up the paperback. "This is the reason you were in here so long?"

"So?"

He shrugged, then set the book upon the edge of the sink. "I should have known. My sisters used to do the same thing."

"Didn't your girlfriends read?"

His eyes twinkled. "Sometimes. But I've never had to help a lady out of her bath before."

"And you don't have to now." But she was getting chilled. Tiny goose bumps dotted her bare arms. "What are you looking at?"

"Your gorgeous little body. I'm also trying to figure out how to lift you out of there."

"Lift me? I just need a shoulder to lean on, I think."

"You need a hell of a lot more than that," he muttered.

"I don't—"

"Hold on," he ordered, leaning over the tub. "I have to brace myself."

"I don't weigh that—" She inhaled sharply when his hands touched her skin. He slid one arm behind her back and under her arm, his thumb grazing the side of her breast. "You can't touch me there—"

"I *have* touched you there," he growled. "Or pretty close." His eyes darkened as he looked at her. Raine was entranced with the raw hunger in his gaze. "And chances are I'll do it again. So shut up and hang on," he ordered, ignoring Raine's protests. "Unless you want to sleep in the bathtub." His other arm cupped the backs of her knees.

Raine had no choice except to put her arms around Alan's neck, all the while hoping desperately that the towel would stay in place.

"I'm going to get your clothes wet," she said.

"That's the least of my problems." He adjusted his grip on her body, lifted her over the edge of the tub and into his arms. "There," he said, sounding pleased with himself. He smiled down at her and then looked at the towel. "It's slipping."

Raine blushed and looked down, grabbing a corner of the towel to keep it in place. "Put me down."

"No 'Thank you, Alan'?"

"Thank you, Alan," she repeated, clutching the towel. "Now put me down."

"Right." He carried her out of the bathroom and across the dimly lit bedroom to the bed, its ivory quilt smoothed neatly into place. He lifted back the covers to expose the flowered sheets underneath, then plopped Raine onto the bed, her head against the lace-edged pillows.

Charlie, curled up at the end of the mattress, lifted his head and growled at Alan.

"Quiet," Raine told the animal. She quickly adjusted the towel and attempted to slip her legs under the sheets, but the weight of Alan's body prevented her from hiding under the covers. "Would you hand me my robe, please? It's on the chair by the desk."

Alan's arms were still around her. "I think I like you better naked."

"Alan . . ."

He bent to kiss her, and she reached for him. She had to admit that she loved kissing him, even though it wasn't the smartest thing in the world for her to do. Raine touched his face, feeling the freshly shaved skin under her palms. He smelled good, too. "Did you have a date tonight?"

"No. I thought I'd get out of here so I wouldn't end up here, in your bedroom."

"What made you think you'd end up in here?"

"Lack of willpower."

"That's not very flattering."

He kissed her lips once again, then lifted his head to smile into her eyes. "Of course it is. Means you're irresistible."

"I'm also naked," she grumbled. "And very embarrassed."

"I prefer it," he murmured, kissing her neck. His hand dropped to the towel. "Your skin feels like silk."

"Apple blossom bath oil."

He nuzzled her neck. "I'll remember the fragrance for the rest of my life."

"You shouldn't say things like that."

"Why not?" He lifted the terry cloth barrier and his lips drifted lower to the top of her breast. "I mean it. I'll remember the feel of your lips and the softness in your eyes when I touch you like this...." His fingertips stroked her breast. "And I'll remember the first time we made love."

"We're not making love," she protested softly.

"We will. If not tonight, then sometime soon." He smiled at her as his hand cupped her breast, and Raine's breath caught in her throat. "I can wait."

Raine wondered if she could. Still, she fought to maintain a grip on her defenses. "You're not the kind of man I expected to—to have in my life."

"I guessed that. I didn't expect you, either."

"I guessed that," she echoed. His lips met hers for a long, searing kiss, until all thoughts of any other kind of man vanished—just like the towel between her body and Alan's. She didn't know how she moved onto her side or how Alan's body came to lie facing hers. She felt pillows drop to the floor, heard Charlie whimpering outside the bedroom door, but nothing mattered except the feel of Alan's hard body against hers, pressing closer, and his mouth, pleasing her, touching her, tasting her.

Finally he released her, but his mouth still hovered above hers. "This is your last chance to send me out in the hall with Charlie."

"Well, we haven't known each other very long." She kissed his chin.

"Not a very long time at all," Alan agreed, sliding his hand along her side, dipping at her waist and lingering at her hip. "But I don't remember ever feeling like this."

"Me either," she murmured, leaving a trail of tiny kisses along his jawline.

Alan grinned. "Stop that. I'm trying to be serious here."

"You can be serious if you want to." Raine smiled, reached for the buttons on his shirt and began to undo the first one. She'd reached the third before Alan took over the job himself.

He moved off the bed and dropped his shirt onto the floor. His chest was bare and tanned, with a tantalizing path of chest hair that disappeared into the waistband of his slacks. "Don't move. I'll be right back."

Raine sat up, keeping the sheet around her, but knew she couldn't move even if someone removed the cast from her leg and paid her a million dollars. But there was still something important to settle between them, before this went any further. "Alan? Wait, I—"

He turned, the planes of his face shaded in the dim light. "I have something upstairs," he said, as if reading her mind.

"You don't have to—"

Alan shook his head. "Of course I do. I always use—"

"There's a box in the bathroom, in the medicine cabinet. I think Claire put it there a few days ago."

"Smart old witch." Alan locked the door and went into the bathroom. He switched off the bathroom light, leaving the room lit only by the moonlight behind the flowing lace curtains.

Nerves fluttered in Raine's stomach when Alan returned to the bed. It was one thing to be lifted out of the bathtub—quite another to be making love with a man who was practically a stranger. But when Alan leaned forward and kissed her, Raine's fears disappeared; the passion between them exploded into something she didn't want to stop, wouldn't stop even if she could. They clung together while he removed the last of his clothing and the pink towel fell onto the floor.

There was no longer a reason to go slow, no longer any way to hold back. He followed her down and onto the mattress, skin against skin, hard seeking soft in a tangle of sheets and pillows. When he would have slowed to touch, explore and caress, Raine slid her hands to his hips and urged him against her.

When she would have taken him inside her, he hesitated. "I want it to be good for you."

"It is," she whispered. "It will be."

He entered her, surely, hard and deep, and her hands slid along his back to hold him close. He thrust slowly, letting her grow used to him. Raine trembled as his lips grazed her neck, found the quivering pulse at the base of her throat and moved to claim her lips once again. She hadn't expected to want him this much.

He made love to her with complete absorption and passionate skill. Raine moved with him, sensing what pleased him, until there was nothing left to hold back. The exquisite tension built until she climaxed around him, holding him in her tight warmth while sensations rocked her body. Answering tremors shook Alan's body, then his hoarse cry touched Raine's lips and took her breath away.

Later, tucked in the curve of his shoulder, Raine wondered what had possessed her. She'd had three dates in as many years, and none had come close to turning romantic in her own brass bed. She hadn't needed or wanted anyone in her life until lately. Had Claire really cast some sort of spell over this summer?

She snuggled up to Alan, pleased with the way he filled up her bed with his large masculine body. Whatever magic had been woven around them, Raine hoped it wouldn't disappear. At least not for a while.

"You have driven me crazy," he groaned.

"What?"

"I've fantasized about making love to you for weeks, since the first time I saw you holding that stupid dog. Raine . . ." He paused, choosing his words carefully. "I never intended to make love to you tonight."

"I know. You were going to the movies."

"Yes."

"What were you going to see?"

"What difference does that make?"

She ran her fingertips along his shoulder, enjoying the play of muscles underneath his skin. "I just wondered."

"I didn't really care. Just as long as it was something violent. Something to take my mind away from wanting you."

"Interesting the way a man's mind works."

"Yes," he said. "Men are very smart. We remember things, important things—like the smell of apple blossoms on a woman's skin."

"Is that what you'll think of when you're back in London or New York or wherever your office is?"

"I don't want to talk about London or anything else right now. I want to make love to you again," he murmured. "Maybe I should stay in this room for the rest of my life, watching your eyes light up when you smile and I'm inside of you."

"You sound more like a poet than a banker," she said.

"That's a compliment, isn't it?"

"Of course. No one's ever told you you were poetic before?"

"No."

"A banker with the soul of a poet," she teased. "That's an odd combination."

"Maybe I could be good at both."

She lifted her head so she could give him a wicked look. "You're good at a lot of things."

"True," he drawled, smiling into her eyes. "I could think of five or six."

Her hand found him, she smoothed her palm across the hard, satin flesh and felt him swell against her fingers. "Shall we start with the first one and work our way up?"

"Sweetheart, I'm beginning to like the way you think."

9

"GOOD MORNING."

Raine opened her eyes to see Alan walk across the room, a mug of coffee in each hand. She couldn't prevent the blush that heated her cheeks as he approached the bed. He wore white shorts and a navy polo shirt and looked as if he were ready to play a few sets of tennis. "Hi."

"I brought coffee," he said, carefully setting the mugs upon the nightstand. "But you can go back to sleep if you like."

"Uh-uh. It smells wonderful." She sat up, bunched her pillows behind her and looked at the clock. "I slept until ten-thirty?"

He handed her the coffee. "We had a late night."

Alan didn't have to remind her. Last night's memories were all too real. Making love with him had been an unexpected pleasure, an experience she would always treasure, even if she wasn't sure how it fitted into the general picture of her life. Raine attempted to sound casual, as if she accepted coffee in bed all the time. "You've been awake a long time?"

Alan sat down on the edge of the bed and smiled at her. "I sneaked out early, before the children woke up."

"Thank you."

"You've very welcome." His smile seemed to mock her politeness.

"Don't tease. I'm not very good at this morning after talk," Raine admitted, sipping her coffee. It was hot and strong, just the way she liked it.

"There are several variations of morning after," Alan suggested, his dark eyes twinkling.

"Such as?"

"The man leaves while the woman is asleep and is never heard from again."

"What if she wakes up?"

"He says he'll call her."

"And does he?"

"No."

"That doesn't sound very nice. What else?"

He reached for his coffee, took a swallow and thought for a minute. "They have breakfast together. They make small talk. If he's still attracted to her, he might panic and start backing off. He says he'll call her."

"And does he?"

"Maybe. It depends."

"Are there any alternatives, such as *she* leaves first, says she'll call and doesn't?"

"It happens."

"None of this sounds like a happy ending."

"You believe in happy endings? I'm shocked." Alan waited for Raine to defend herself, but she merely drank her coffee. "Of course, I haven't mentioned one other scenario."

"Which is?"

"He has pursued—and won—the woman of his dreams, and wild horses couldn't tear him away from her side."

Raine laughed. "In fairy tales, maybe, but not in real life."

Alan shook his head. "What am I going to do with you, sweetheart?"

"Help me take a bath?"

He stood up beside the bed. "If that means that I can get my hands on your body again, then of course."

"I don't think the children would understand."

"I rented five movies this weekend. They won't even leave the television set."

"That's not good for their eyes."

"It's ninety-nine degrees already, it's Sunday, and the tourists have jammed traffic all over the island. I don't think that this once we need to worry about their eyes. In fact, they're well taken care of. Everyone has had breakfast and the kitchen is cleaned up. All I have to do is take you to the tub."

She set her empty cup upon the table, swung her bare legs over the edge of the bed, then realized she was naked and her robe was still across the room. Fortunately the sheets were tangled, so she grabbed one and preserved her modesty. She tested her foot on the floor, leaning part of her weight upon it to see how it felt. Some soreness, but not much. She looked up; Alan was hovering close to her.

"You're an amazing man," she said, making a face at him. "But I can't figure you out."

"You don't have to," he said, swinging her into his arms. "I have everything figured out for both of us."

Raine was afraid he was right.

SUNDAY PASSED in a haze of heat, sunlight, secret glances and shared smiles.

Alan offered to move the air conditioner into Raine's room, for the fortieth time, and she refused once again.

Raine insisted on helping cook lunch, and Alan took her up on it. She sat at the kitchen table and grated cheese, while he fried the hamburger for the taco filling. The children spent a quiet day watching movies, then ate Popsicles and played games on the shaded back porch. Donetta listened to the radio, hoping to win tickets to the Michael Bolton concert in Providence, and beat the twins at Monopoly. Vanessa, Crystal and Julie spread dolls and doll clothes all over the living room while Toby complained that there was nothing to do.

This was what it would be like, Raine realized, watching Alan pile food onto paper plates. This was what it would be like if they were a real family. If these kids were really hers and if they had a real father.

If Alan stayed. Raine hardened her heart. She was thinking like a love-struck idiot, when she was a mature woman who should be able to handle a summer love affair.

"ARE YOU SURE everyone's asleep?" Raine whispered.

Alan opened the refrigerator and took out a bottle of white wine. He set it upon the table in front of her. "You don't have to whisper. And yes, I'm sure."

"Good."

"That's an understatement." He winked at her and pulled the foil from the top of the bottle. "This foster father business is wearing me out."

"This isn't the vacation you had planned."

"But I think it's the vacation Claire and Edwina planned." He poured the wine into glasses and handed one to Raine. "Here. The best California has to offer. And not in a paper cup, either."

"Thank you."

"Drink up. I'm going to ply you with alcohol and then make love to you." Alan kept his voice light, but his body hardened at the thought of having Raine beneath him once again.

She didn't look concerned. "Is that how bankers seduce women?"

"Hey!" He touched her glass with his. "Whatever works."

"Last night was . . ." She hesitated, and Alan's heart stopped beating.

"Was what?" he asked carefully, concentrating on loosening his death grip on the fragile crystal. He watched her take a deep breath and he braced himself.

"Incredibly...special," Raine answered. "But I don't want you to think that *I* think it . . . meant anything."

"You don't want me to think *what?*" In the interest of safety he set the glass down. *What the hell was she talking about?*

Raine drained her glass. "You know what I mean."

"No," he answered through gritted teeth. "I don't."

"You don't have to get angry about it." Her eyes were very large and very blue as she looked at him. Alan was glad there was three feet of pine separating them. "I just wanted you to know that—"

"Our making love didn't mean anything," he finished for her. "Is that right?" She had the gall to nod. He wanted to wring her neck. "It meant something to me."

"It's temporary."

"I know." He frowned. "But that doesn't make it meaningless."

"I don't know why you're getting so upset. We're mature adults. Neither one of us has any commitments," she began.

"Honey, the last time I counted you had *seven* of them."

"Don't interrupt." She took the bottle, refilled her glass and took a sip. "This is really wonderful wine."

"Don't change the subject. You were talking about commitments?"

She turned her gaze back to him. "Yes. Maybe I phrased that badly. Neither one of us *needs* any more commitments." Her grin was lopsided. "Is that better?"

"Yes." He finished his own glass. "But what's your point, Raine?"

"I just wanted you to know I understood that."

"Well, that makes one of us." He would never understand women, not even after growing up with four sisters. "Drink up, sweetheart, because I want your body."

"I want yours, too."

That was all he needed to hear. Alan kicked his chair back and stood up, reaching for Raine's hand. He lifted her to her feet and kissed her, his lips insistent on her warm skin. She lost her balance, and Alan gripped her shoulders to keep her from falling, but didn't move his lips from hers. His hands slid to her waist, feeling the tempting curves underneath the cotton shirt, and lifted her onto the counter.

"Spread your legs," he whispered, and as she did, he stepped into the V between her thighs.

The cotton barriers between them were the most exquisite torture Raine had ever known. She wrapped her arms around Alan and pulled him closer, and his tongue played with hers as heat burned lower and centered between her legs, where his body was pressed so intimately against her own.

She'd thought she'd melt when his fingers teased a trail along her thighs, then higher, to slide under her baggy shorts.

She was so glad she was wearing baggy shorts.

His fingers gripped the tops of her thighs, holding her legs open while his thumbs caressed her burning skin, teasing the edges of her nylon panties, turning her legs to butter and her skin to fire.

"We can't do this here," she moaned; his thumbs caressed the moist scrap of fabric until she felt as if she wasn't wearing anything at all.

"But we are," he countered, his lips finding her earlobe and tugging gently on the soft skin.

Raine groaned and reached for the buttons on his shirt. "We shouldn't. Someone could come in."

"I locked both doors," he whispered, sending shivers of need through her body as he eased his lips under the collar of her shirt.

"Do you always think of everything?"

"I do my best," he admitted. Raine finished unbuttoning his shirt and slid her palms across his hard chest, loving the feel of his skin under her hands. "Now yours," he demanded, keeping his hands high on her thighs, his thumbs continuing to create a heat Raine no longer wanted to deny.

"This is crazy." She unbuttoned her shirt and released the front clasp on her bra, pushing the fabric aside to invite him to move his heated skin against hers.

"We could go to the bedroom," she whispered, at the same time wondering if her knees would hold her if she tried to jump down from the counter. She reached for the waistband of his shorts and released the clasp.

"Too far away."

He was right. Raine didn't want to wait to feel him inside her. Her fingers hurried to find the zipper tab and tug it downward. His mouth melded with hers again, a hot, arousing kiss that raised the temperature in the kitchen to a record high. "What about the kitchen table?"

"Next time," he promised, leaving Raine with erotic visions of future August nights.

"The floor?" She slid her hand under the elastic waistband of his underwear, wanting to do what he was doing to her. Her fingertips touched the hard length of him, feeling the taut, heated satin; Alan groaned.

"Tomorrow," he said, his breathing ragged as he lifted his mouth from hers. He slid his hands down her thighs and away, leaving her with an empty longing.

She wanted him inside her, wanted that delicious, hard length of him filling her.

She didn't care anymore how he did it or where. Nothing mattered except wanting Alan, loving Alan. It didn't surprise her when he pushed one of the legs of her shorts high, when his fingers tugged the damp scrap of satin aside, when he moved into her and filled her with such pleasure that it took her breath away.

When she gasped he claimed her mouth, his tongue moving with hers, her breath catching in her throat as he took her. She wrapped one leg around his waist, holding him to her, and urged him deeper. Her clothing seemed to capture him inside her. It was wild and hot and frenzied; she had never felt such crazy need in her life. Perspiration ran between her breasts, slick against Alan's chest, as she gripped his shoulders. He filled her, thrusting again and again with such raw need and power that Raine could no longer deny her body's greedy reaction. She tightened around him, felt him pull the very climax from deep in her body until endless spasms shook her. Shook them both.

He lifted his mouth from hers, and Raine could feel the bruising her lips had taken. His arms cradled her, but neither moved. Or could move. Raine felt the rapid pounding of his heart under her breast and knew he could feel hers in equal rhythm. For long moments they clung together in the dim light of the kitchen, neither willing to move.

Raine put her head upon his shoulder and willed her heart to slow its beat so she could pull away, pretend this was only a brief interlude of heated sex and not the dangerous, illogical behavior of a woman in love.

CHARLIE BARKED at the front door when a black limousine pulled up in front of the house. Raine peered out of the living-room window and saw a plump, middle-aged lady dressed in black step from the car. She watched in amazement as the chauffeur took three bags from the trunk and followed the tiny woman up the sidewalk.

Charlie yapped in unison with the doorbell, bringing Alan from the kitchen while Raine, barely limping, went to answer the door. Alan hurried past, taking the suitcases and setting them inside.

"I won't need you for another hour, at least," Alan told the uniformed man. He nodded and strode down the steps.

The gray-haired woman stood patiently. "Mr. Wetmore Hunter?"

"Yes. You must be Miss Minter."

Her sweet, round face burst into a radiant smile. "Wonderful of you to send for me! I told Mrs. Alex it was so lovely of you. Of course, Mrs. Alex's brother would have to be lovely, now wouldn't he?" She turned to Raine as if seeking confirmation.

Alan spoke first. "She means my sister, Alexandria."

Miss Minter's gaze went past Alan's shoulder toward the staircase. "Oh, these must be the little lambs! Hello, duckies!"

"Duckies?" Raine looked at Alan. "What's going on?"

"What's a duckie?" Joey asked.

Jimmy was not about to be outdone by his twin. "Are you from another country?"

"England, my dear. A very long time ago." The children came down the stairs and gathered around the tiny woman. Her head barely topped Donetta's. "Why don't you show me where your kitchen is and we'll cook up something for breakfast?"

"Come on." Julie took Miss Minter's hand. "Where's England?"

Joey rolled his eyes. "Don't be such a dope, Julie. Everyone knows where England is."

"Come, come," Miss Minter clucked. "We mustn't call each other names. I'm Miss Minter, and that's what you shall call *me*."

With that, she led the children down the hall, the eight of them chattering together happily as they headed toward the kitchen.

"Alan, who was that woman?"

"Miss Minter. Isn't she wonderful?"

"Answer my question first. Who is she?"

"The new housekeeper."

"I don't have an *old* housekeeper."

Alan looked very pleased with himself. "You have one now. I called Alex days ago, and she promised to help me find someone who could take over running this household."

"I run this house."

"Not lately. And not on one leg, you don't. Besides, I thought you would enjoy a little time off."

"This is my job, Alan. I can't afford to hire someone to take care of things around here. People like that cost a fortune."

"You don't have to worry about that. I've taken care of everything."

"In other words, you just have to wave your check-book around and everything falls into place."

"I don't know why you're so angry."

"If you didn't want to help with the kids, you should have told me. If you were sick of it you should have packed your bags and left."

"I didn't—don't—feel that way. But I've got work piling up upstairs. And the children can't continue to eat hot dogs off paper plates for another week or two, and if you go back to walking around here full-time, your foot is going to take forever to heal. I thought sending for help was the best solution."

"You should have discussed it with me first."

"I wanted to surprise you."

"Surprise me? This is my house, my children. And my problem."

"It's been my problem, too, or haven't you noticed? I can't stay here indefinitely—we both know that." With that, he pushed open the screen door and went onto the porch.

"I don't want her to stay!" Raine called, hurrying after him. She didn't want to think about him leaving. "You hired her, you tell her to leave."

"No way." He stopped and smiled at her. "We need her."

"I don't—"

"Need anyone?" He kissed her lips briefly, then shook his head. "Of course you do. You just haven't realized it yet."

"ARE YOU FALLING IN LOVE with him?"

Raine's heart sank. Her stepmother would never leave the subject alone. "Who I'm in love with—even if I'm not—is none of your business, Claire."

"Of course it is," her stepmother replied. "Whose business would it be?"

"Mine." Raine glared at her foot as she rocked in the porch swing.

"How is your foot, dear?"

"Much better. It hardly hurts. I'm going to call that doctor and see if he will take the cast off sooner."

"When do you think you'll be up to dancing?"

"Dancing? Are you kidding?"

"No, darling, I'm not." Claire took a pad and pen out of her purse. "I'm planning a party. A birthday party."

"It's not your birthday. In fact, your birthday is in November."

"Close enough." Claire shrugged. "Besides, I feel like celebrating early."

Raine decided not to try to figure out Claire's logic. She'd always been a little strange about birthdays. "All right. I'll ask the doctor when I can dance."

"Can't you tell for yourself?"

"Okay. I hardly limp, unless I've been walking around for a long time. I'm sure I could dance, at least a little."

"In ten days? There was a cancellation at Rosecliff— I love the ballroom. The bride called off the wedding. I have to make definite plans and let them know to-day."

"Claire, do whatever you want. Just write the date on my calendar, if it means that much to you."

"I want it to be a special evening."

Suspicious, Raine glanced at her stepmother. "Special for whom?"

"You and—"

"Don't say it. What's between me and Alan is none of your business."

"None of my business? I *sent* him to you! You should be thanking me, you should—"

"Should not speak to you," Raine finished.

"Why? He's wonderful."

"Yes, right now he is. Because he wants to be. He's on vacation and it's a lark to play uncle to seven children. He's made it clear that this isn't his kind of life-style, not permanently."

"And what do you think he's playing with you? House?"

"I don't know. He hired a housekeeper without telling me, and he's sending the kids back and forth to camp in a limousine, for heaven's sake."

"A stroke of genius."

"You would agree with him."

"What good is having money if you don't use it to make your life easier? Why should he spend his time wiping noses when he can hire someone to do it for him?"

"Is that how my father looked at parenthood—as wiping noses?"

"You have a blind spot where your father is concerned. I loved that man, so watch what you say about him."

"He loved you, too." Raine smiled at her stepmother. "I always thought that was the nicest thing, even though I probably wasn't very kind to you at first."

"I thought you were, darling. So serious and scared."

"That house wasn't fun until you arrived."

Claire beamed. "What a lovely thing to say! Your father was good for me, too. I wasn't used to staying in one place. Your father settled me down, gave me a place to call home. Opposites attract, they say." Claire pulled a linen handkerchief from her purse and dabbed her eyes.

Raine thought of her weekend making love with Alan and couldn't disagree with Claire. Despite their differences, they'd made a lot happen in a few short days. It terrified her. She'd fallen in love with him, which was the stupidest thing she'd ever done in her life.

"Anyway, I think you've fallen in love with Alan Hunter, even though you don't want to admit it," Claire declared. "It's made you cranky. A party is exactly what you need to lift your spirits."

"MISS MINTER?" Raine peered into the kitchen and was amazed by the transformation. The floor sparkled, the table gleamed with fresh polish, and the counters were cleared of dirty dishes and clutter.

"In here, duckie!"

Raine followed the sound of the lady's voice into the laundry room and saw Miss Minter sorting clothes.

"Here, I'll help with that," Raine said, feeling guilty that someone else was sorting her dirty laundry.

"The little lambs are very lucky, aren't they?"

"Lucky?" Raine started a pile for blue jeans.

"To have a home like this, and a sweet girl like yourself to love them and take care of them," she declared. "I didn't hesitate a bit when I heard about them." She winked at Raine. "Retirement is no fun, my dear. No fun at all."

"Do you mind my asking where you came from?"

"Heavens, no! One of those little retirement places in Florida. God's waiting room, they call it. Now I know why. Thank the good Lord Mrs. Alex called me. I took care of her husband's family, you know. Worked for them for years. Mrs. Alex wanted me to help with her little ones, but I thought I might be too old for babies. My hearing isn't as good as it used to be." She smiled again. "I can hear your children, though. They speak up quite well, now, don't they?"

"Uh, yes, they do. How long are you able to stay?"

"Just as long as you need me, duckie." She switched on the machine and shut the lid. "Just as long as you need me."

That was the trouble, Raine decided, going back into the gleaming kitchen. She needed too much all of a sudden.

How could she fire Miss Minter? She needed someone with two good legs to deal with the children. How could she bear to think of Alan leaving? She needed his arms around her at night—or any other time, for that matter. And Claire? She could tell her stepmother to mind her own business, but Raine even needed Claire's antics to cheer her up. Still, she needed to back off a bit. Self-preservation.

Alan poked his head in the door. "Still angry with me?"

"No. I'm sorry I yelled. I don't like surprises."

"You're allowed. I should have asked you first." He looked around the kitchen and whistled slowly. "It pays to hire the best, doesn't it?"

"I still can't believe it," Raine groaned.

"Are you talking about sending for Miss Minter or what happened on the kitchen counter last night?"

"Both, I guess."

"Me, too." He came over to her and kissed her, pulling her into his arms.

"Miss Minter is in the laundry room," Raine warned.

"Okay. The counter's safe, for now."

"The bed wasn't bad, either."

He grinned and attempted to slide his hand under her shirt. "Not bad at all."

Raine stopped him, unwilling for the housekeeper to find them groping each other. "Tell me about the chauffeur. You hired him, too?"

"His name is Harry, and yes, I hired him, too."

"That's a waste of money. I have a perfectly good van in the garage."

"Someone else can deal with Newport traffic," Alan explained. "I have better things to do with my time."

"Such as?"

"Come upstairs to my room and I'll show you."

"I can't," Raine said, smiling at him. "Your mother and Claire will be back any minute to discuss their party."

He swore under his breath. "They're back?"

She nodded. "Claire came by a while ago, after you stomped off."

"I didn't stomp off. I walked down to the Wave café for breakfast."

"Whatever. They're planning a little party and have rented the Rosecliff ballroom."

"Why?"

Raine decided to protect her stepmother's privacy. "For Claire's birthday party. I have a feeling it's going to be very fancy and very romantic."

"Romantic? I like the sound of that."

"They hadn't given up, you know. They're still matchmaking."

"I'm not complaining."

"You should be," Raine said, before his lips touched hers. When the kiss ended, she stepped back. "This has gone too far, Alan."

He let her go. "How?"

"The bathtub, the bed, the *kitchen counter*, for heaven's sake. I'm not used to . . . behaving this way. I think I should go back to wiping noses and you should go back upstairs and do whatever it is that you do."

"I hired Miss Minter so you would have some time off."

"No, you hired me so that *you* would have time off." She shook her head when he would have protested. "Let's take a break, okay? You're going back to London soon and I don't want to get hurt." Raine didn't know how much clearer she could be.

Alan hesitated before he spoke again. "Fair enough. I'll go back to being the boarder, but we have a date for Claire's ball. Fair enough?"

"Yes." She wouldn't admit, even to herself, that she'd already fallen in love. There was nothing fair about that.

10

"WHO'S THE SMARTEST friend you have, Edwina?"

"Martha VanDoorn," the tiny woman replied from the neighboring chaise lounge Maizie had so thoughtfully provided for their comfort.

"*Martha VanDoorn?*"

"Last year she won eleven thousand dollars on Wheel of Fortune."

"That doesn't count." Claire sniffed. "I'm not talking about *buying vowels*, for heaven's sake."

Edwina held out her glass and Claire poured another martini from the pitcher placed conveniently on the table between them. "You're talking about the party, I suppose?"

"I'm talking about matchmaking, Wina. The party will create the perfect evening for romance. Our children won't be able to resist each other. I have it all planned. Raine will wear a lovely Halston I just happened to see downtown, and of course your son will look outrageously handsome in a tuxedo. Don't forget to remind him to send for one."

"I won't."

"And also remind him about flowers."

"I will." Edwina took a delicate sip of her drink. "These martinis aren't as good as the ones Miss Minter makes for us."

Claire agreed. "She's a gem. That was a stroke of genius on *your* part."

Edwina was pleased to have received a compliment from her friend. Claire didn't give compliments often. "Well, dear, I have my moments."

"I've never understood how you raised five children, though."

"With a housekeeper, a cook and a nanny, of course. While you were traveling all over the world with your first husband, I stayed in New York having babies."

"I envied you," Claire said with a sigh. "Roland never wanted children."

"Well, it's a good thing you divorced him and married John Claypoole. You ended up with Raine and Quentin."

"And I love them dearly. So much that I can't bear to see Raine living her life alone."

Edwina reached out and patted Claire's hand. "Now, now, darling. We've taken care of that, haven't we?"

"No, you're not going to get out of it."

Edwina winced. "Now, Alan..."

"Don't use that maternal voice on me, either." Alan took his mother's elbow, led her onto the front porch and guided her to the swing. "Sit."

"Of course, I'd love to chat with you," Edwina began, her hands fluttering uselessly in the air. "But the three little girls are waiting for a story and I promised..."

"They can wait a little longer," Alan said, sitting down beside her. He planted his feet on the floor to prevent the swing from rocking and turned to his mother. "What is this crap about a party at Rosecliff?"

"Well, it was Claire's idea...."

"Don't give me that innocent look, Mother. You and I both know it won't work."

"Well . . ." She sniffed. "*Sometimes* it does."

"You're matchmaking with that woman. You've never meddled in my life before, until now."

"And it's about time, too." Edwina smiled at him encouragingly. "Claire and I thought a little party might be just the thing to make you and Raine see each other in another light."

"I don't get it."

Edwina shrugged, as if to say *Men!* "It's supposed to be romantic, darling." It was time for a little white lie. "I've noticed that Raine isn't exactly falling in love with you."

"That is my business."

"Well, is she?"

"I don't know."

"Well, there you have it. You need help."

"Mother, I don't know how you got into all this in the first place, but you and Claire arranged for me to rent these rooms, didn't you?"

"Of course."

"Because you thought I'd be a good husband for Raine?"

"Yes." She wagged a finger at him. "And I know you need a wife. My father's will was very specific."

"I can't believe the old man was allowed to make a will like that."

"It wasn't so unusual in that day and age. My father was a little eccentric, but he held strong opinions and he lived by them."

"Couldn't anyone talk him out of it?"

"Whatever for? Darling, you were just a small child. Men and women married young in those days. They certainly didn't wait until their mid-thirties, for heaven's sake. Who would have known that it would cause this much trouble?"

"It's caused a great deal of trouble," Alan declared, thinking of the lawyer's fees he'd paid over the past eighteen months, and so far all for nothing.

"Marry the girl, Alan. You're in love with her. I can see that without your having to tell me."

Alan opened his mouth, but no words came out. How could he deny something that was staring him in the face? And what on earth did he want to do about it?

Edwina patted him on the cheek. "Close your mouth, darling. You'll be all right in a moment."

Alan took a deep breath. "Don't get your hopes up, Mother. Raine and I are as different as night and day."

"You have to convince her that you're the perfect man for her, my dear. With more than words, of course."

"WELL?" Raine twirled on the landing. "What do you think?"

Anything Alan hoped to say stuck in his throat as Raine paused on the staircase. Seven children surrounded him and watched the black-haired beauty in the shimmering pink dress walk toward him.

The twins started a war whoop and the rest of the children joined in, even Vanessa.

"You look like a princess," Julie declared. "Like in a book."

Donetta held the Instamatic camera and focused it. "Smile," she ordered. Raine stopped on the bottom step and did as she was told. The flash popped and Raine turned her gaze toward Alan.

"You look very impressive," she told him. He looked very nonchalant and elegant, as if he wore tuxedos every day. She'd certainly been to many parties with tuxedo-clad men, but somehow this was different.

Tonight was different.

She couldn't put her finger on it, but something special was happening. Raine met Alan's admiring gaze and tried not to blush.

"It's true," he murmured, taking her hand and lifting it to his lips. "You do look like a princess."

"Thank you." Her skin burned where his lips had touched.

Raine felt like one, too. She'd argued with Claire about the gift of a dress until she saw what Claire had purchased. In the end, as Claire had known would happen, Raine hadn't been able to resist. With the strapless bodice trimmed with silver accents, its elegant simplicity was just too tempting.

"Shall we?" Alan held on to her hand as if he was afraid she would disappear forever if he let go.

"I want a picture of the two of you together," Donetta said. "Everybody get out of the way."

The rest of the children reluctantly moved away from Raine so the couple could smile obligingly for the camera, then Raine knelt to hug the children. "Everyone be very good for Miss Minter, okay?"

"'Kay." Crystal yawned.

Jimmy sneezed, Vanessa hid behind Alan's legs, and Toby looked upset.

"Are you comin' back?" he asked, his brown eyes dusted with suspicion.

"Of course we are," Raine promised, suddenly realizing that this was the first time since they'd moved in that she'd left Toby and Crystal at night. "But it will be very late, so we'll see you in the morning."

The little boy nodded and sidled up to Joey, who tried to reassure him. "We'll watch a movie and eat popcorn," he told his friend. "We'll have fun, you'll see."

"And so will we," Alan said, tugging Raine toward the door.

Harry stood at the curb, the limousine door open for them. As they approached, Harry presented Raine with a large spray of white roses tied with a silver bow.

"They're beautiful," Raine said, touching the velvet petals with gentle fingertips.

"White roses seem to fit you," Alan murmured, helping her into the car.

"Thank you," Raine said, setting the bouquet upon the opposite seat. "You didn't have to do that."

"I know I didn't. It's something I should have done weeks ago."

Raine didn't know what he meant by that, but she didn't pursue it. "You didn't notice anything different?"

"What? Your hair looks the same to me."

"It is the same."

"The diamond earrings are stunning."

"A birthday present from my father many years ago." She crossed her legs in a deliberate motion. "But that's not what I'm talking about."

Alan glanced down to see that silver sandals decorated her feet. "The cast is gone." He looked up at her again and smiled. "When did that happen?"

"This morning. The doctor told me to be careful with how much dancing I did tonight, but he didn't see any reason to keep a bandage on it." The dress deserved more than flat sandals, but Raine wasn't going to complain.

"Congratulations," he murmured, bending close to her ear. "How does it feel?"

"Wonderful," Raine breathed as his breath tickled her ear.

"I've missed you."

"I needed to slow down." She'd tried to give herself time to fall out of love with Alan, but that plan hadn't worked. Just looking at him every day was enough to make her heart beat faster. Not making love to him had only made her want him more.

"I know, but these past ten days haven't been easy." His lips grazed her cheek and then brushed her lips softly. "Did you miss me at night?"

"Yes, but Charlie kept me company."

"I would have gladly kicked him out of your room. I've done it before, remember?"

She shook her head and looked into his eyes. "That was a weekend of . . . madness. I've come to my senses and you should, too."

"You're always telling me what to do," he chided, kissing his way to her other ear and sending shivers along Raine's skin.

"I thought it was the other way around."

He lifted his head as the limousine came to a stop in front of an enormous, white mansion. "See? We're good for each other."

She shook her head and laughed. "I'm not so sure about that."

"I'll do my best to convince you, then."

Rosecliff's wrought iron gates were open to admit Claire's guests, and Raine and Alan stepped inside the white-marbled vestibule. Alan presented his invitation to a butler, who bowed and waved them forward.

Raine slipped her fingers through Alan's as they passed the heart-shaped staircase, with its red carpet and iron railing, into the crowded reception room. Music poured through the wide doors and conversation hummed everywhere. Raine didn't recognize anyone, although several older women nodded politely.

"We'd better find Claire and let her know we've arrived," Alan said, guiding Raine toward the ballroom. "She'll hunt us down if we don't."

"You make her sound like such a witch."

"Isn't she?"

"Not all the time." *Unless she's casting spells, like the one I'm falling under tonight.*

"Watch yourself. You're mellowing."

She was mellowing, all right. Wearing a beautiful evening gown and diamond earrings could have that effect. If that wasn't enough, stepping back into the early 1900s would be the crowning touch. "There they are," she said, waving toward the west wall of the lavish white ballroom where Claire and Edwina were receiving guests. "Holding court."

"Why am I not surprised?"

He wove through the crowd, keeping a careful grasp on Raine's hand. Dressed in antique white lace dresses, Claire and Edwina stood amid a fragrant bank of white hydrangeas, roses, orchids and lilies of the valley. Silver bows decorated the flowers, and matching silver threads sparkled in the ladies' dresses.

"Well, darlings," Claire trilled as they approached, "you're right on time. And the two of you look absolutely wonderful."

Alan released Raine's hand and touched her on the back, urging her toward her stepmother. Raine kissed the cheek Claire offered. "So do the two of you." She turned to Alan's mother. "Hello, Edwina. Where did you find dresses like that?"

"They've been in the family for years," Edwina confided. "My mother never threw anything away."

Alan looked around the room. "Who are all these people? Two hundred intimate friends?"

Claire tapped him on the arm with her fan. "I don't know most of them myself, but I think they're having a wonderful time, don't you?"

"Yes," he said, surveying the crowd. "But how did you convince two hundred strangers to attend your birthday party?"

Edwina answered instead. "It was genius. An absolute stroke of genius. You wouldn't believe what she did."

Alan smiled. "Maybe we would."

"'Stroke of genius' is a bit of an overstatement, Wina." Claire shrugged. "I simply contacted the local Make a Wish foundation and offered to throw a ball. These lovely people bought tickets, and all the money goes to finance fulfilling the dreams of ill children."

"Why, Claire . . ." Raine began, touched by her stepmother's thoughtfulness.

"It's nothing," she demurred, shaking her head slightly. "So darlings, what do you think of my *Ball blanc?*"

Edwina lifted her cheek for Alan's kiss. "She modeled it after Tessie Oelrich's white ball in 1904, right in this very ballroom. Isn't that a breathtaking idea?"

"It's absolutely gorgeous, Claire," Raine agreed. She couldn't help teasing her stepmother. "It's another stroke of genius. You've done wonders in such a short time."

Claire beamed, obviously pleased with Raine's approval. "Oh, yes, I know." She and Edwina exchanged a smug look. "It's one of my specialities."

"LOOK AT THEM." Edwina sighed. "So perfect."

"Yes. Just as we imagined." The conspirators watched the tall, dark-haired man and the tiny, dark-haired woman dance in each other's arms against a backdrop of arched French doors and silver pots filled with flowers. The enormous chandeliers sparkled above the crowd as Claire and Edwina strolled around the outer edges of the room.

"This must be the most beautiful ballroom in Newport," Claire added.

"My grandmother used to tell stories about the balls here." Edwina adjusted the lace on her sleeve. "I never dreamed I'd celebrate your birthday here."

Claire made a face. "I suppose I have to pretend to enjoy my cake."

"I think that would be a nice touch, dear."

"I'll do it later," she promised, hoping Wina would forget. There was enough food and refreshment in the reception room to satisfy the most discriminating palates, so she needn't feel guilty about delaying the cake. Claire kept a careful watch on her stepdaughter between greeting acquaintances and nodding to strangers. She and Edwina paused again when they had another clear view of their favorite couple.

"The rose dress was an excellent choice."

"Your son is playing the part of the perfect gentleman."

"He's not playing a part, my dear. Alan is truly in love."

"Did he tell you?"

"He doesn't have to tell me in words. A mother knows these things."

"And Raine loves him, too."

"Do you really think so?"

"Yes, I do. But the question is, will she admit it?"

ALAN HELD RAINE in his arms and they waltzed to the strains of Strauss. Somehow he knew Claire had selected only the most romantic music for the evening. He was unreasonably and illogically pleased. It fitted his mood.

Tell the woman you're in love with her.

It wasn't that easy, even though he'd had days to examine how he felt about her. He'd missed her body, of course. But he'd missed other things as well. He'd attempted to concentrate on work he shouldn't have been concerned about, while Raine had immersed herself in the children's activities.

Tell her you've fallen in love. The top of her head barely came to his shoulder, her cheek grazed his lapel. Her perfume, some light scent she'd worn before, wafted into his nostrils and drove him crazy with desire. Which, he supposed, was exactly what perfume was supposed to do.

Well, it was working. *Tell her you love her.* Alan's hand tightened around Raine's waist.

"Raine?" he tried.

She looked up, her blue eyes sparkling. "Isn't this fun?"

He promptly forgot what he was going to say. "Yes," he managed.

A little wrinkle appeared between her eyebrows. "Aren't you having a good time?"

"Why would you think that?"

"It's not like you to be quiet," she replied. "You usually have something to say and you haven't said a word for three waltzes."

"Have I told you how beautiful you look tonight?"

Her cheeks flushed. "Yes. And thank you."

Have I told you how much I love you? "It's true," he growled, pulling her close to him. "Do you want to stop for a while?"

"No. I'm not tired and my foot doesn't hurt and I could dance all night in this beautiful ballroom."

"I guess that answers my question." He twirled her in front of the open French doors as a cooling breeze drifted from the ocean. "But I think people are beginning to leave. Claire's birthday party is almost over."

"She loved it. I loved it." Raine gazed into his eyes. "I'm going to dream of crystal chandeliers and champagne tonight. What will you dream of?"

"That's a leading question, sweetheart."

She laughed. "I know. You looked so serious, I had to tease you."

Serious? He was serious, all right. "I don't intend to dream tonight, because I'll be making love to you until dawn. I've had enough of this separation."

"Until dawn? It's after midnight now."

He pulled her tighter against him. "Which doesn't give us much time."

"Only four or five hours."

"Not nearly enough." Raine melted as he looked at her with passion in his eyes. She'd managed to resist the physical attraction between them for almost two weeks, but this was too much. The night, the music, and Alan's masculine charm had all combined to work an irresistible magic around her. She couldn't fight it any longer and didn't want to. The summer would be over soon enough, Alan would return to London, and Raine would return to her seven children.

Life would return to normal. A very lonely normal life, Raine was afraid.

"Would you like some champagne?"

"We'll have some later," she promised.

"Later?"

"At dawn."

ALAN UNDRESSED HER in the semidarkness of the bedroom. He stood behind her and released the zipper, then kissed the nape of her neck and the soft, ticklish place where her neck sloped to her shoulders. He slid the heavy dress down her body, Raine wriggled out of it and draped it over the desk chair. She stood naked, except for thigh-high, sheer stockings and ivory silk panties.

Raine turned to face him, her breasts brushing the tiny pleats in his shirt. He took her into his arms, hummed something that resembled a waltz, and danced her slowly around the dark room.

"I didn't know you were so romantic."

"I told you that you didn't know me very well," he murmured, tucking their clasped hands to his chest. His fingers brushed her breasts and sent tingling shocks along her bare skin. "You don't even know that I've fallen in love with you, do you?"

"No."

"Are you in love with me, Raine?"

"Yes. But I didn't want to be," she confessed.

"I know." His hand tightened on the smooth curve of her waist.

She smiled at him. "Then how do things like this happen?"

"Coincidence. Fate. Magic." He stopped dancing and bent to touch his lips to hers. "I don't know which one," he said before he kissed her. It was a kiss full of love and promise and longing, and Raine felt as if she would shatter into tiny pieces from sheer happiness. Somehow she managed to unbutton his shirt and he shrugged it off his shoulders. She fumbled with his clothing in the darkness until she was the only one left with anything covering her body. He was hot and hard against her as his lips sought a trail along her neck and moved down to tease her breasts. He knelt before her while his fingers eased the tiny scrap of silk over her abdomen and along her thighs in a slow motion. The whispering trail of silk glided down her thighs to her ankles, until Raine lifted her foot and kicked the garment aside.

He treated her thighs the same way, caressing her skin with his lips as he slowly removed each fragile stocking. When he stood once more, Raine, trembling and needy, reached for him and held his hard length in her hands. She smoothed the satin skin and marveled that there could be such passion in her life, in her bed, in her body.

Alan groaned and swept her into his arms, carrying her the few steps to the waiting bed.

He made love to her with his hands and mouth and with all the words he hadn't yet spoken.

She made love to him with her fingertips and her lips and with all of the love she'd stored in her heart.

And when he joined his body with hers, when he filled her and she held him, they moved together in a timeless rhythm of love and passion, until the world exploded into shards of crystal, shimmering through the ebony night.

"MARRY ME." Alan lifted his head from the pillow and peered at Raine. Her eyes were closed, her breathing was even and soft. She lay cuddled against him, her round backside pressed against his groin in a most satisfactory way. Alan cleared his throat and tried again, this time a little softer. "Marry me."

It wouldn't hurt to practice, he decided. He moved strands of dark hair from her cheek. "Marry me," he whispered into her ear, hoping she would awaken and put him out of his misery.

But Raine didn't move, not even an eyelash. It was growing lighter as dawn greeted the room. He knew he should slide out of bed and tiptoe up three flights of stairs before Miss Minter or the children woke up, but he didn't have the heart to leave Raine yet.

He wanted her to open her eyes and smile. He wanted to make love to a sleepy woman on a Sunday morning. He wanted the scent of apple blossoms on his pillow at night, he wanted to hear her laughter in the afternoon. He wanted her to marry him and stay part of his life forever, because he couldn't imagine spending the rest of his life without her.

Alan put his head upon the pillow and closed his eyes. He would let Raine sleep as long as she needed. He would still be here when she woke up.

RAINE HEARD THE SOUND of little footsteps hurrying down the stairs and pulled the sheet over her head to block out the noise. She started to stretch, but her toes bumped someone's warm shins.

Alan.

Raine opened her eyes and struggled to wake up. Alan shouldn't be here. But he was, snoring softly near her ear, his larger body warm against hers. She wouldn't, shouldn't explain this to seven little children on a Sunday morning. Seven little children who always brought her the Sunday paper and climbed into bed to fight over the comics.

Charlie whined at the door and Raine groaned. The little dog wouldn't give up until he got into the bed. He scratched and whined louder, until Raine was afraid he'd bring all the children to the door, worrying that something was wrong.

She slid carefully out of bed, tiptoed to the door and unlocked it. Then, hiding behind the door, she opened it enough to let the dog inside before locking it shut behind him. Charlie gave her a pained look, trotted across the room and jumped onto the bed. Raine hurried after him, afraid of what the little dog would do when he saw Alan.

But Charlie just padded up to Alan's face, sniffed and turned away to return to the foot of the bed.

"Good dog," Raine whispered.

"Mmm?"

Raine climbed back into bed and pulled the sheet over her. She touched Alan's rough cheek and smoothed a lock of dark hair from his forehead. "Nothing. Go back to sleep."

He opened his eyes. "Did that damn dog just kiss me?"

"Sort of. That's what happens when you don't go back to your own room."

"I'll risk it." He slid a warm palm over her skin. "I'll risk it anytime."

"Well, I won't. We have to sneak you up the back staircase."

"Couldn't we have coffee first?"

"Later."

He kissed her shoulder. "Then couldn't we make love before you send me away?"

Raine snuggled against him. "The children will be knocking on the door any minute now. I heard them downstairs a few minutes ago."

"Marry me, then."

Raine froze. "What?"

He smoothed her hair and looked into her eyes. "I'm serious, Raine. Marry me. Let's wake up together for the rest of our lives."

"Alan..."

"You know I love you. And you've said you loved me."

"I do," she whispered.

"Then spend the rest of your life with me."

"I can't..."

"Yes, you can. Just say yes."

Her heart resumed beating with a rapid pounding, and Raine took a deep breath while Alan waited for her answer. "I can't," she finally stammered again.

"Will you think about it?"

"What are you asking me to do, Alan?"

"It was a simple question."

"No, I don't think it was." Raine eased herself out of Alan's arms, away from the warm comfort of her bed. Minutes later, safely behind her locked bathroom door as the shower spray soaked her skin, Raine blinked back tears. Marry Alan? It wasn't simple at all. Was he asking her to give up her home? Her job? Her children? Was she supposed to pack up and follow him to London, host parties in fancy gowns and attend charity luncheons?

She'd seen that life. It was her mother's life and Claire's, but it wasn't hers.

11

"LET ME TRY asking you again," Alan said, entering the kitchen. Raine missed the tuxedo, but at least this was the man she knew, one in beige slacks and a jade polo shirt. He came to the table and smiled at her. "By the way, you look beautiful in yellow."

"Thank you." After her shower, Raine had changed into a bright sundress and drank two cups of coffee, all in hope of taking her mind off Alan's proposal. Nothing had helped, she realized, but at least now she was wide-awake.

Alan sat down beside her at the kitchen table and pushed two empty cereal bowls out of his way. "No comment?"

"If it's about what you asked me an hour ago, I wish you wouldn't," Raine pleaded as he leaned closer. "Someone could walk in at any minute."

"If they do, I'll change the subject," he promised. "Why won't you marry me?"

"I think I need some more coffee," Raine said, rising from her chair and heading to the other side of the kitchen.

"Not a good enough answer. I'll take you out for breakfast," Alan offered. "We can talk privately and you can have all the coffee you want."

Raine hesitated, unwilling to discuss marriage in the middle of the kitchen, while Miss Minter folded clothes in the next room and little girls played dolls on the back porch.

"Besides," he continued. "Edwina and Claire could drop in anytime now to recap last night's party. Maybe you don't want to miss their visit."

"You're playing dirty."

"Yeah."

The last thing Raine needed this morning was Claire's scrutiny. She'd seen the triumphant expression on her stepmother's face when they'd left Rosecliff. "All right."

"We'll walk to La Forge," Alan said, looking pleased. "They serve brunch on the porch."

Raine told Miss Minter where they were going, then stepped outside with Alan into the sunshine and headed down the street toward Bellevue Avenue, where traffic was already heavy. Alan held her hand while they walked the three blocks to the restaurant.

"This will be over after Labor Day," Raine said as they dodged the crowds.

"I may have to go to New York next week," Alan said. "But I'll be back within a few days."

"You're certainly well rested now. Your vacation was good for you."

He smiled at her. "Yes, in many ways."

"When do you start back to work?"

"I haven't decided yet. I need to make a decision soon, though." He pushed open the heavy wooden door and ushered Raine into the restaurant's cool darkness. "A lot depends on you."

She wished her stomach wouldn't drop to her toes at the thought of him leaving. She loved him, but couldn't live with him. And he knew it, too, despite all his masculine insistence to the contrary.

They walked down the narrow hallway to the other end of the restaurant, where a hostess showed them to a small table near the window overlooking the grass court. A jazz quartet played a bossa nova in the middle of the porch, lending a festive mood to Sunday morning.

After they'd ordered coffee and the waitress had told them to help themselves to the buffet in the other room, Alan turned back to Raine. "Now, where were we?"

"Could we have coffee first?" As if on cue, the waitress stepped to the table and filled their cups, giving Raine no more excuses.

"Why won't you say yes?"

"Why do you keep asking?"

"Because I love you." He smiled at her again. "And I don't give up easily."

"I know. That's why you're still living in my house."

"Right. You're beginning to understand me."

"No. I don't understand you at all."

"But last night you said you love me—or was that just passion speaking?"

Raine looked around, hoping no one could hear them. Fortunately none of the other people in the room were paying the least bit of attention. When she turned back to the man waiting for an answer, she couldn't help hearing the love in her voice. "Of course I love you."

"Of course," he repeated, shaking his head. "But not enough to marry me."

"Not enough to give up everything I've worked for, everything that's important to me."

"I wasn't aware I had asked you to do that." He frowned at her and, realizing they weren't making any progress, stood up. "Come on. Let's call a truce and have breakfast."

During breakfast they discussed the weather, the summer, the traffic, music, his sisters and her brother. He revealed he spoke three languages. She confessed her love for country and western music.

He asked her to marry him in German, French and Russian.

"Stop," Raine demanded, setting her empty plate aside for the waitress. "You're teasing about something important."

"Well, at least you admit it's important. This morning you flew out of the bed in the middle of my proposal. At least here you've had to stay in one place long enough to listen to what I have to say."

"What are you asking, Alan? What role does the wife of Alan Wetmore Hunter, international financial wizard, play? What do you expect of me?"

"Just love, sweetheart."

She shook her head. "Nothing's that simple, and you know it. Would we live in London? Would we have to travel? Entertain?"

"Not necessarily."

"Could you be more specific?"

He took her hand. "I can't, not until I've met with people in New York next week. All I'm asking is for a chance to work it out together."

"What about the children?"

"Raine, I love what you do."

"I can't take them with me." Her eyes filled with tears. "If I leave with you I leave them, too."

"Don't make me into a monster. I'm not asking you to leave the children."

"You're not?"

"No. Marry me, the sooner the better, and we'll work out the rest."

"There's more to this than you realize." Raine took a deep breath. "Julie and the twins are going to be up for adoption soon. Are you ready for instant fatherhood?"

"You're going to adopt them?"

"If the state agrees."

He leaned back in his chair. "I admit, it would take some getting used to, but . . ."

"But what?"

"I'm not shaking with fear, if that's what you mean. We can work this out, Raine."

She wanted to believe everything was as simple as Alan thought. She wished she could fall into his arms and give him the answer he wanted. "What do you want me to say, Alan?"

"I'd prefer a yes, but how about a maybe?" He smiled at her and held her hand tightly within his.

Raine allowed her romantic little heart to hope. After all, he hadn't run screaming out of the restaurant. Maybe he'd grown more accustomed to family life than she thought. "Okay. I'll definitely think about it. But you have to think about this, too."

He smiled at her, a smile full of promise and confidence. "How could I think of anything else?"

"THAT'S THEM coming down the road, isn't it? What's going on, Claire?"

She stood at the door and peered out. "I don't know."

"Why, Claire!" Edwina gasped. "I don't think you've ever said that before."

"They don't look as happy as they did last night." She turned away from the screen and shrugged. "I think they've reached some sort of crisis."

"*Crisis?*" Edwina wrung her hands. "They're supposed to be falling in love, not having a *crisis!*"

"Shh! They're coming up the walk now. You don't want them to hear you shrieking." The two women arranged themselves on the porch swing and picked up sections of the Sunday newspaper.

"Hello, ladies," Alan said as he opened the door and he and Raine stepped inside. "Enjoying your Sunday?"

"Very much, darling." Edwina lifted her cheek for his kiss. "Did you enjoy the party last night?"

"Yes," he replied and turned to Claire. "It was certainly an evening to remember."

"That's what I'd hoped," Claire replied, watching him with narrowed eyes. If there was a crisis going on here, this young man could certainly hide his feelings. She would never find anything out from *him*.

Edwina held out the sports section. "Would you like part of the newspaper?"

"No. You'll have to excuse me, ladies." He moved towards the door. "I have some packing to do."

"Packing?" his mother echoed, but Alan had already gone into the house.

Claire turned back to Raine, who sank into a wicker chair like a wilted yellow flower. "Something wrong, darling?"

"I'm just tired." She avoided Claire's curious gaze and looked at her watch. "It's almost noon. Miss Minter has the rest of the day off, so I'd better change my clothes. I think I'll set up the sprinkler in the backyard. The children would like that."

"We could go to Bailey's," Claire suggested, determined to spend the afternoon with her stepdaughter and discover what was going on. "I still have my membership."

"No beach for me today. The sprinkler in the yard will do just fine." Raine stood up and smoothed her skirt. "Besides, it's about time things around here went back to normal."

After she'd left, Edwina turned her anxious gaze toward Claire. Newspapers slid off her lap and onto the floor, but neither noticed or cared. "He's packing, and she's talking about going back to normal. I don't like the sound of that. I don't like the sound of that at all."

"*Back to normal*," Claire scoffed. "That's the silliest thing I've ever heard."

"Oh, I agree," Edwina said. "We've never been *normal* in all of our lives."

THE REST OF SUNDAY passed peacefully, so peacefully that Edwina and Claire finally grew restless and returned to Maizie's. Alan stayed upstairs in his air-conditioned retreat. Miss Minter went to the movies with an old friend she'd discovered summering across the bay.

Raine played in the sprinkler with the children, squirted them with the hose to make them shriek, fixed chocolate milk shakes and egg salad sandwiches for supper, and at sundown tucked seven sleepy children into their beds. It was dark before her foot began to ache; she walked through the silent house and into the kitchen for a cold drink. The Sunday crossword puzzle and Charlie waited on her bed.

Alan, naked to the waist and wearing shorts, closed the refrigerator and set a platter of leftover ham upon the counter.

"Hi," he said when he saw her. "I was going to look for you. I made reservations on the early-morning shuttle to New York."

Her heart skipped a beat. "Oh?"

"It's perfect timing. You wanted time to think and I need to make plans. I'll be back in a couple of days, so don't give my room away."

"I won't." Raine told herself it was foolish to feel so disappointed.

He opened the wrapping on a loaf of bread. "Want me to make you a sandwich, too?"

"No, thanks," she replied, stepping up to the counter to watch what he was doing. "I'm going to bed."

Alan turned to her and touched his lips to hers. "I take it that's not an invitation."

She shook her head. "Sex just confuses things."

Alan looked at her, an amused gleam in his eyes. "Sweetheart, if that's true, then we must be the two most confused people in Rhode Island."

IT WAS WEDNESDAY afternoon before Raine finished cleaning the house. Miss Minter had been a big help— she had to admit it—but no one person could keep up with seven small children and all of the chores involved in keeping a house clean.

She'd given Miss Minter a few days off, knowing the kindhearted lady would never leave unless Alan told her it was all right to do so. It felt good to be back at work, to be able to fix breakfast, stop squabbles, braid Vanessa's hair and take the children to camp. It kept her from missing Alan too much.

All seven children had complained when Alan left. He'd promised to return, which they'd tried to believe. They'd all heard too many false promises to believe one more, no matter how much they longed to.

Raine wanted to believe, too. This summer hadn't been what she expected, that was certain. From the time Alan Wetmore Hunter appeared on the doorstep, her life had been turned upside down, no matter how hard she'd tried to resist. She could have done without Claire and Edwina's interference, and maybe she could have resisted Alan if she hadn't torn the ligaments in her foot and needed a bath, but Raine wasn't positive. Miss Minter and Harry and a magical evening at Rosecliff were part of a summer that would never be forgotten.

The summer when she fell in love.

The summer when she fell, period. She sat on the couch, flexed her foot and wiggled her toes. Almost as good as new, thanks to everyone's help. She didn't know what she would have done without Alan. She missed his teasing. She missed his body beside hers in the night. If she married him, how would he stay here? Would life go on the way it had for the past few weeks? She'd dreamed it would go on like this forever, until they were old and gray and rocking on the front-porch swing. Perhaps they'd plot romances for their grand-children and watch the happy endings from a discreet distance. When he returned, Raine decided, she'd let him ask her again.

And this time her answer would be yes.

"IT'S OFFICIAL."

"What is?" Raine cradled the telephone receiver against her ear and took a box of Popsicle ices out of the freezer. She counted out seven and passed them out.

She motioned to the children to take them out to the backyard so she could talk to Mindy privately.

"I've spent all day in court and just returned to the office, but I wanted you to know—the judge terminated parental rights for the three kids."

"Thank goodness. Will you tell them or shall I?"

"I will. I'll be down next Friday, if that works out for you. We need to talk about this, Raine. I need to know if you're thinking about adopting them."

"I don't think I can bear to let them go."

"That's not the same thing. Do you want to be considered?"

Raine looked out the screen door and saw the kids sitting in the shade of the elm tree. "More than anything, but *could* I adopt them?"

"Legally, as their foster mother, you have that right. Since they've been with you so long, staying with you would be seen as in their best interests. Can you handle it?"

"I handle it now."

"True, but you're a single woman. A young single woman. Is this something you want to do? And I have to be honest, Raine. Those children, especially the twins, have been without a father all of their lives. I think they need one."

An image of Alan running out of the surf with two little boys behind him popped into her head. Yes, they needed a father. What child didn't? "They'll have one, Mindy."

"Oh?" Mindy's voice lost its official tone. "Are you trying to tell me something?"

"Unofficially. I can't go into it now." *Not until Alan returns and we settle everything.*

"The handsome houseguest, right?"

"Right." Raine turned around as Claire, holding Charlie in her arms, stepped into the kitchen. "Give me some time to get things straightened out here, okay?"

"You've got all the time you need."

The trouble was, she needed a lot more than time. She needed Alan to return and tell her he was going to stay with her forever, children and all.

"What was that all about, darling?"

"Joey, Jimmy and Julie," Raine said, trying to sound nonchalant. "They're going to be available for adoption. I knew it was coming—their social worker has been trying to get a court hearing on this for ages—but I guess I wasn't as prepared as I thought."

Claire sank into a kitchen chair, the dog still in her arms. "I can't picture them anywhere but here."

Raine leaned against the counter. "Neither can I."

"They'll need a father, too," Claire reminded her. "Especially as they get older."

"I know." Raine smiled to herself. The dream was becoming more real all the time, but she didn't dare tell Claire until she and Alan had talked.

"Alan's in love with you."

"Yes."

"And you're in love with him."

"Yes."

"Good. He'll be a wonderful father for those three children."

"You're getting ahead of yourself."

Claire shrugged. "Perhaps. What's going to happen to the others?"

"I don't know," Raine admitted. "Vanessa is making progress and isn't as bashful as she used to be. At one time the state thought they'd located a grandmother, but I haven't heard anything since. Donetta's social worker thinks she's found an aunt who wants custody, but it will take a while for the home study to be done. Toby and Crystal just entered state care, so no one knows what's going to happen to them. That's seven lives, Claire. Seven lives to think about and take into account when a man like Alan tells me he loves me."

"Eight lives," Claire said, "counting yourself. And what do *you* want?"

"I want it all—Alan, the children, everything," Raine answered. She smiled an upside-down smile. "Do you think it's possible, Claire?"

"If you believe in yourself—and each other—then anything's possible, darling. Anything at all."

"SHOULD WE TELL HER?"

Edwina hesitated at the front door. "I don't know, Claire. It could be risky."

"It could be just the thing, too. One never knows in matters of the heart."

"You may be right, but perhaps Alan should be the one to tell her. After all, it's his—"

"Tell me what?" Raine asked, pushing open the door so they could enter. The two ladies exchanged nervous glances, then looked back at her.

"How about a martini?" Claire suggested. "I think we could all use a drink."

"I don't drink martinis," Raine said. "I hardly ever drink. Besides, I'm making dinner."

"We'll keep you company," Claire offered. "Where's Miss Minter?"

"She'll be back tonight. I gave her a couple of days off."

"Was that wise, dear, considering your foot and all?"

"My foot is perfectly fine. I was waltzing in the Rosecliff ballroom, remember?"

"And beautifully, too," Claire agreed.

"Did Alan say when he'd return to Newport, dear?"

"He said he'd only be gone a few days. Maybe he'll call tonight."

"Maybe he will."

Edwina began. "Claire told me about your predicament with the children, dear. I hope you don't mind."

Raine poured spaghetti into the pot of boiling water and picked up a wooden spoon. "That's okay."

"We have a possible—"

"Claire..." Edwina was fluttering again. "I still don't think..."

"We have a possible solution," Claire went on, unaffected by her friend's stammering. "Go on, Wina. Tell."

Edwina opened her mouth, but no sound came out. Raine stirred the pasta until it softened, then turned the heat down. She looked at Edwina. "Would the two of you like to stay for dinner?"

"That would be lovely," Alan's mother said, brightening. "Perhaps the children would like to hear a story while you're cooking. I could go—"

"Tell her now, Edwina."

Raine set the spoon upon the counter and turned her full attention on the women. She was beginning to grow accustomed to their fractured conversations.

"Well, Claire said you need a husband. A father for those children, so you can adopt them."

"Well, it's not that simple." Raine wished she could tell them that she and Alan were going to go along with their matchmaking plans permanently. Where was Alan, and why didn't he come home?

"That's the lovely part of all of this," Edwina said, her face bursting into a smile. "Alan needs to get married, too! He needs a wife."

"Look," Raine said, holding up one hand as if to stop Edwina's unbelievable words. Why would Alan need to get married? "This isn't—"

"Oh, yes, it is," Claire insisted.

Edwina looked confused. "Is what?"

"Any of your business," Raine said gently. "Even if I believed you."

"Of course it's my business." Edwina sniffed. "I'm his mother. Whose business would it be but mine?" She pointed to the steaming pot. "You'd better stir."

"Thanks." Raine did as she was told, wishing for the hundredth time that Alan was here to help control the ladies. Their schemes had gone too far this time.

Edwina leaned forward. "Now, here's the best part. Listen carefully. Alan really does need a wife. It's in the will."

"What will?"

"His grandfather's. It's very complicated, dear, but Alan can't inherit my father's estate unless he's married. The property reverts to the state at the end of the year, and of course no one wants to see that happen because they'll put a road through it."

Raine stopped worrying about sticky spaghetti and faced the two women. "Alan *needs* a wife?"

Edwina nodded. "Yes! See how easy this is! Almost as if it were meant to be. You need a husband, even though you didn't need one before, of course. But now you do!"

Raine struggled to understand the meaning behind Edwina's words. Surely she couldn't have heard correctly? "Is this why Alan came to Newport?"

"Oh, yes. He wanted to talk to the lawyers in person, but he couldn't accomplish a *thing*. They simply told him to get married."

"*Who* told him to get married?"

"Atwater, Brenner and Horton."

Claire nodded. "Of course, that idea was totally ridiculous until he met you, darling."

"Totally ridiculous," Edwina repeated.

"What's totally ridiculous?"

At the sound of Alan's voice, the three women froze into silence and saw Alan enter the room, Charlie growling at his heels. "Hello, ladies. I thought I'd find you here." He smiled and loosened his tie before stepping to the stove to kiss Raine.

She managed to resist throwing her arms around his neck. "I didn't know you were coming back tonight," she managed to say.

Alan frowned. "I wanted to surprise you, so I had Harry pick me up at the airport. What's wrong?"

Claire and Edwina stood up and picked up their purses. "We'll just be going, darlings."

"Oh, no, you don't." Raine glared at them. "You can't just drop a bomb like this and then tiptoe away."

"What bomb?" Alan said, looking at his mother, then at Raine.

She stared at him, wondering if she knew him at all. Was this another trick Claire had conjured up to throw them together? Could she have been so wrong? "Claire and Edwina have been telling me a story about your grandfather's will. Is it true?"

Alan frowned again, at his mother this time. "What's going on here?"

Raine spoke before Edwina could explain. "We've been discussing our marriage, Alan. Or rather, your marriage. Is it true?"

"Is what true?"

"I told her about Father's will," Edwina whispered. "I thought it would help."

"Is it true you need a wife?" Raine repeated, willing him to say it was another crazy matchmaking scheme. She couldn't possibly have fallen in love with a man who would use her as a legal loophole. He couldn't be that good an actor, but then again, what did she know?

"Yes. That's why I came to Newport, but it doesn't have anything to do with us."

"Sure it does," Raine declared, hardening her heart against those warm, hazel eyes. Her fingers shook as she lifted the spoon to stir the spaghetti. She had to remember she had a family to feed. "Especially if *I'm* supposed to be the wife."

"Raine..."

"I've decided I don't need a husband, after all, so I'm not accepting your proposal." Raine looked into the face of the man she loved and felt her heart break into jagged pieces. Suddenly it was hard to breathe. "The answer is no."

12

CLAIRE GASPED. "You mean he's asked you already?"

"Yes," Raine said, tearing her gaze from Alan's frown. "Last weekend."

"I think we've made a slight miscalculation," Claire whispered. She grabbed Edwina's arm and attempted to get her out of the kitchen.

"The answer is no?" her son repeated. "Just like that? *No?*"

"Yes," Raine told him. "And dinner is ready."

"I don't give a damn about dinner." He moved out of the way of the steaming pot as Raine lifted it toward him. "I just want to know what the hell is going on around here."

She smiled sweetly as she passed him on her way to the sink. "I've finally come to my senses, that's all. Would you tell the children to come inside for dinner?"

"No."

"Fine. I'll do it myself." She set the pot into the sink and started toward the back door. "Hey, everybody!" she called. "Time to wash up for supper!"

Alan turned back to Claire and Edwina, who were attempting to sneak out of the kitchen. "Where are you two going? And why isn't Miss Minter cooking dinner?"

Raine answered for them. "I gave her a few days off. She deserved it."

"I think she's here now," Edwina trilled. "Charlie's barking at the front door."

"I'll be right back," Alan muttered.

When he'd left the room, Raine looked at the two women and shook her head. "Don't say a word."

Claire looked worried. "Darling, I'm not sure this will business is why he wanted to marry you."

She shook her head. "Don't be so sure, Claire. Somehow everything is beginning to make sense."

Raine didn't know how she made it through dinner, or why she'd served spaghetti and meatballs. By the time the meal was finished, the children looked as if they'd bathed in tomato sauce. Claire and Edwina escaped before dessert, claiming a prior date at the movies with Maizie Chapman.

Miss Minter, undisturbed by the chaos, told the children stories of her girlhood adventures in Liverpool with one of the Beatles' mothers until they'd finished their dinner.

"I still don't know what's going on around here," Alan muttered, standing up and waiting for Raine to leave the table with him. "But I'm damn sure going to find out. Come on."

"No," Raine stated, rising to her feet. She hoped she could make it to her room before tears overwhelmed her. Now that the shock was wearing off, she didn't know how she would be able to control herself. "There isn't anything else to say." She turned to Miss Minter. "Would you mind overseeing baths and putting the children to bed without me? I'm not feeling well."

Miss Minter nodded. "No problem, duckie. You take good care of yourself."

"Raine, wait!" Alan moved toward her.

"Good night, everybody," she said, then hurried to her room and locked the door before Alan could catch up with her. She turned on the faucet over the tub, hoping the rushing water would drown the sound of her sobs. What had she done? She'd thought Alan really loved her. Well, she should have known better. Great sex had clouded her judgment.

We'll work it out had been his words. Now she understood. Working it out had meant he'd get what he wanted, what he had come to Newport to accomplish. No wonder he hadn't minded adopting the children. He hadn't intended to be around long enough for that to matter, one way or another. Besides, he'd hire whomever he needed to deal with them.

Everything had happened so fast. Now she knew why.

ALAN STOOD OUTSIDE Raine's closed bedroom door until he felt a tug on his hand. Julie peered at him. "What's the matter, Mr. Hunter?"

"I wish I knew, honey."

"We're going to have ice cream. Miss Minter said."

"Sounds good."

"Want to have some?"

Alan took the child's hand. There didn't seem to be any other choice but to leave Raine alone. "Okay."

"Want to hear a secret?" Julie motioned to him to bend down. "We're gonna be adopted."

He didn't have any idea what he should say. "You are?"

She nodded. "Joey heard Raine talking to Grandma Claire about it. Raine's gonna be our mom."

Alan straightened, still holding Julie's sticky hand. He let her tug him down the hall, but his mind was whirling.

He'd thought Raine loved him. Now he wasn't even sure about that.

"RAINE! You have to come out sometime," Alan called. "The kids have to leave for camp in ten minutes, and I need to be back in New York by eleven."

"Go."

"Not until we talk." He jiggled the doorknob. "I don't know what kind of game you're playing, but I'm not into it. Open this damn door or I'll take it off the hinges."

"It's no game," Raine said, opening her bedroom door and backing away as he entered the room.

"Since when do you think you have to lock your door?"

"I needed some time to think." A long, sleepless night had given her the hours she'd needed to decide how to say goodbye to Alan.

"And?" He stayed on the other side of the room.

"We need to start being honest with each other."

His eyebrows rose. "I won't argue with that. Are you going to tell me what happened yesterday?"

"Why did you suddenly decide to marry me? It wasn't because you realized you couldn't live without me, was it?" She crossed her arms in front of her chest and wished she had dressed before letting Alan into her room.

"If I said yes, you wouldn't believe me, anyway." He sat down on her unmade bed.

"I was going to say yes," she muttered. "I thought we'd be one big, happy family." This was no time to tell him she loved him. She wouldn't admit she'd been a fool. "And then I found out you have a small legal problem. You need to marry before you can inherit your grandfather's estate. How am I doing so far?"

"You have your facts straight."

"I thought so." She waited for him to defend himself. Waited for him to tell her he loved her, that this whole thing was a ridiculous misunderstanding. Waited for him to take her into his arms and make this nightmare disappear.

He stood up, his face expressionless. "Is there anything else?"

She shook her head, tears clogging her throat so she couldn't speak. *Tell me you love me.* A muscle clenched in his jaw, but his hands were gentle on her shoulders as he kept her facing him.

"Are you through?" he asked.

She nodded. "You can go to New York now."

"No way. It's my turn." He looked down, holding her gaze. "It's easy to believe the worst, isn't it? That I would marry you for money." He took a deep breath before continuing. "I'd do a lot to keep my grandfather's house—in fact, I've spent a small fortune in legal fees to do just that—but I wouldn't get married for it."

"But . . ."

"No, just listen. You've had your chance to talk." Alan dropped his hands and turned toward the window. "I don't know why an old man made a will the way he did, but I'll be fighting it for years."

"That doesn't seem fair," Raine said.

Alan shrugged and shoved his hands into his pockets. "That's not the point, is it?"

"No."

"Sweetheart, you didn't want to believe that what we felt for each other was real. You didn't want to take a chance by loving me, so you jumped at the first thing that got in our way."

"That's not true."

"No?" He shook his head, as if he couldn't believe she'd deny it. "You were waiting for an excuse, Raine. You're so afraid of loving me, needing *me*, that you couldn't wait to find something, anything, to believe it wouldn't work out."

"Raine?" Donetta's voice came from the hall. "We're going to camp!"

"I'll see you later," Raine called. "Have fun!"

Alan waited until the front door slammed shut and the house grew quiet. "Those kids out there are a lot braver than you, sweetheart. At least they give people a chance. No matter how screwed up their lives have been, they're willing to love again."

"And what about those kids, Alan? What would I have done with them if I married you? Tossed them back?" She blinked back tears as she stared at him.

"Is that what you think?" She didn't answer, so he went to the door and put his hand upon the knob. "You asked me once if I avoided getting involved with women because I played it safe." He shot her a rueful smile. "I thought you hit a little close to home on that one."

"I never meant to hurt you."

"No, it was true. I had played it safe. Until I fell in love with you and gave you everything I had to give— and you didn't notice. I got pretty involved with this family, too. Or didn't you notice that, either? Well, sweetheart, I'm not the only one playing it safe around here. You'll hide in this house, not risking a thing, in-

stead of sticking your pretty neck out and trusting me."
He shook his head and his smile was wry. "You're right
about one thing, Raine. You don't need anyone. You'll
always do just fine by yourself. I just hope someday,
when you wake up, you don't regret the choices you've
made."

Raine watched in silence as Alan opened the door
and left the room, shutting the door behind him with a
careful, final click. She listened to his footsteps disappear down the hall, but didn't move. She stood there
as if turned to ice, wondering if the numbness in her
body would ever leave.

"WE'RE RESPONSIBLE," Edwina moaned, wringing her
hands as she faced Claire in the limousine. "We have to
do something."

"We will," Claire assured her. "I have to give it more
thought."

"More thought? He's been gone three days! And
Raine hasn't spoken a word to either one of us since that
horrible spaghetti dinner. Miss Minter says she's been
very quiet with the children, too. What do you think
happened?"

"It doesn't take a genius to figure out that they had a
disagreement."

"A disagreement! He's flying back to London this
week, for heaven's sake! Right after the hearing."

Claire sat up straight. "What hearing?"

"About the will, of course. On Wednesday. The anniversary of my father's death. I told you I ordered
special flowers for the grave site and—"

"Alan's coming to Newport?"

"He has to." She frowned. "At least, I think he does."

"You're going to call him and tell him he has to, Edwina. Tell him it's some legal problem you don't understand, but it's very important."

Edwina chuckled. "You're thinking up something clever, aren't you?"

"Of course I am. Now all I have to do is figure out what to do about Raine."

Edwina patted Claire's arm. "You'll think of something. You really *are* the smartest of all my friends."

"YOU CAN'T JUST SIT around the house and mope."

Raine ignored her stepmother and plugged the vacuum cleaner cord into the outlet. "This place is a mess."

"So is your life, darling."

Raine looked up, exasperated. "I really don't need this, Claire. Miss Minter went to pick up the kids from camp, Jimmy's upstairs asleep because his asthma is acting up again, the social worker just left, and I have a lot on my mind."

"Like what?" Claire bent down and put Charlie into her lap. "How would I know what you're thinking about? You haven't talked to anyone in days."

"Which has been a pleasant change, believe me."

"I don't believe you." She patted the place beside her on the couch. "Come here. You look like death. You're not eating, are you?"

"It's too hot," Raine lied. Food stuck in her throat when she tried to swallow. She left the vacuum cleaner in the middle of the floor and joined Claire on the couch. She knew her stepmother wouldn't give up until she'd said what she came to say.

"There," Claire said, turning to face Raine. "This is much better. Did the worker come to discuss your adopting Julie and the boys?"

"Yes."

"What are you going to do?"

"I don't know." She hugged her knees to her chest. "I love them and I want to keep them, but is it fair?"

"If it makes all four of you happy, then that's what matters."

"It isn't that simple."

"You shouldn't have sent Alan away."

Raine didn't know whether to laugh or cry. "He sent himself away."

"Because of the children?"

"No. He said that I was so afraid of loving him that I was waiting for an excuse to believe it wouldn't work out between us. He was so angry with me, and he had a right to be. I thought he just wanted his grandfather's property, not me."

Claire looked as if she wanted to cry. "You never really trusted him, did you? You thought he was too much like your father."

"Isn't he?"

"No. Your father was not a demonstrative man. He held his feelings inside, dear, but he did have feelings. He should have spent more time with you and Quentin, should have given more of himself, but he did the best he could. Maybe he would have lived longer if he hadn't worked so hard."

"He loved his work. He didn't love us."

"No, darling. I'm afraid that's a bit simplistic. And unfair, too. Your father just didn't know any other way."

"And Alan does?"

"If I were you, I'd give it a lot of thought before I lumped your father and Alan Hunter in the same category."

"It doesn't matter. It wasn't the happily-ever-after romance you and Edwina had envisioned. Alan isn't Prince Charming, either."

"Prince Charming? You wouldn't recognize Prince Charming if he waltzed naked across your bedroom."

Raine closed her eyes against the memory of dancing with Alan in her room. "Stop it, Claire."

"Wake up, darling. Happily ever after doesn't simply *happen*, my darling. Two people who love each other *make* it happen."

"We're not talking about love, Claire."

"We're not?" She put Charlie onto the floor and stood up, brushing dog hair from her navy skirt. Then she reached for her purse and opened it. She handed a packet of photographs to her stepdaughter. "I had these developed for Donetta. Look at them and tell me we're not talking about love."

Raine took the envelope and lifted the flap. She looked through them until she came to the pictures taken on the staircase before the ball. Alan and herself stared back at her, giddy expressions of love on their faces. Identical, love-struck expressions. No one could fake that kind of radiance.

Claire touched Raine's cheek. "If you love those kids, keep them. If you love Alan, take a chance and go after him."

"It's too late, Claire. He was furious."

"He'll get over it."

"I can't go to New York."

"You don't have to." Claire looked at her watch. "He's in Newport for the reading of the will. Edwina said he's driving to Boston afterward and catching a plane to London."

Excitement curled in the pit of her stomach. "He's here now?"

"Until four. Which gives you twenty minutes."

"I can't leave . . ."

"Of course you can. Take the limo. I'll stay here in case Jimmy wakes up."

"You'd do that for me?"

"Darling, I'd do anything to make you happy."

Raine looked at her worn denim shorts and wrinkled, blue shirt. "Do you think I have time to change?"

"Definitely, darling." Claire hid her sigh of relief. "Put on some makeup and wear something white."

"Here we are, miss." The driver stopped the car in front of the brick entrance to the historic Hotel Viking.

"I thought we were going to the law office," Raine said.

"Yes, miss," he agreed. "But first I have to pick up something for Mrs. Claypoole."

"Is it going to take very long?"

"No, miss."

Raine waited for the chauffeur to return, grateful for the extra minutes to question her sanity. What on earth was she doing? Was she wrong to put her faith in a couple of photographs? What could she say that would make Alan stay? What if he didn't want her, after all? What if he wouldn't even speak to her? What if—? Suddenly the possibilities were overwhelming. She breathed faster, unable to stop herself from worrying.

Feeling faint and dizzy, Raine leaned over and put her head between her knees, hoping the blood would come back to her head and she could tell the driver to take her home. This was not the best idea she'd ever had.

The door beside her opened, letting a blast of muggy heat hit her legs. A familiar voice said, "What the— Raine?"

She tried to lift her head, but the dizziness returned. "Alan? Oh, my God."

"What are you doing here?"

"Hyperventilating, I think." She heard him ask the driver to go inside for a bag of ice.

"Don't move."

No chance of that. Her legs had gone numb, whether from nerves or hunger she didn't know. "What are *you* doing here? You're supposed to be at the lawyers' office."

"That particular meeting ended an hour ago. My lawyers bought me some more time."

"Then it's not too late?" Raine dared to hope her stubbornness wouldn't cost Alan his inheritance. "You can still inherit the property?"

He didn't answer. "Why are you here, fainting in the limousine I ordered—?"

"I know—to take you to the airport. To London," she moaned.

"London?" He brushed her hair from her face. "I'm not going to London. Who told you that?"

"Claire. She gave me the car to use, too."

"My dear mother sent this car for me. She said Claire had taken care of everything."

"Here we go again." She should have known Claire and Edwina wouldn't give up so easily.

"Can you lean back? I have the ice."

"I'll be okay. I think the heat got to me." And the sleepless nights and a sporadic diet of Cheerios and Snickers bars. Alan put the bag of ice against her forehead, and Raine closed her eyes and let the cold soak into her skin. "This is so embarrassing."

"I know."

"This isn't the way I had it planned."

"Move over," he said, sliding into the seat beside her. His thigh touched hers, but Raine didn't mind the heat. "Had what planned?"

"Finding you. Saying I'm sorry. Telling you that were right—I am a coward. I *was* a coward. At least I'm trying not to be. Not anymore."

Alan shut the door and spoke to the driver. Then he put his arms around Raine, all the while keeping the ice pack on her head. "Sweetheart, are you trying to tell me something?"

"Yes." Then she felt the car move. "Where are we going?"

"A few miles north of here, to Portsmouth. I'm going to show you my grandfather's estate." His arm tightened around her. "Just close your eyes and take deep breaths until we get there."

She did as he instructed, grateful for the quiet minutes and the cold blast of the air conditioner. When she felt the car slow down, she took the ice pack away and opened her eyes. The car had stopped in front of an enormous field. Several black-and-white cows chewed grass behind the weathered fence.

"This is it?" Raine asked.

"That, too." He pointed to a mammoth barn and the tiny house that sat in front of it. "My grandfather made a lot of money in his lifetime and he married a woman with even more, but he never forgot where he came from. Two acres of rocky farmland isn't worth much, not even to developers. There's no ocean view. The state of Rhode Island wouldn't mind getting their hands on it, though, in case they want to add another highway."

"But you won't let them?"

"I'm going to try." He leaned forward. "Back to the Viking," he told the driver. Then he looked down and replaced the ice pack on Raine's forehead. "You look better. Are you sure you're okay?"

"Why are you being so nice to me?"

"I'm always nice to women I plan to marry. I'm not—"

She moved the ice aside and stared at him. "What did you say?"

"I'm not going to London," he continued. "I'm not leaving the country or even the island, for that matter. I don't give up that easily."

"But your work—"

"Can change. Can be done from Newport. I've spent a lot of time in New York, arranging things the way I want them."

"They let you?"

He looked surprised. "It's my company. You never did know me very well."

Maybe not, Raine realized, but she had the rest of her life to take lessons. "I'm learning."

"Good. The first thing you'll learn is that I don't make decisions based on money. There are other important things in life, sweetheart."

She reached up and caressed his cheek. She wondered if it was possible to burst with happiness. "Like what?"

"Like spending the rest of my life making love to a woman who lives in an old house with a bunch of kids and a dog who looks like a cat."

Raine smiled, remembering Alan's protests. Had it really been only a few weeks ago? "A woman who thinks every man who knocks on her door has been sent by her stepmother to marry her?"

"Yeah," he replied, pulling her into his arms. "That's the one."

JULIE SQUIRMED on the couch next to Vanessa. "What happens next, Grandma Claire?"

Claire turned the page of the storybook, and all of the children waited quietly to hear her read. "The prince took the princess into his arms and kissed her, a long and tender embrace that caused the flowers to change from gray to red, the birds to sing a sweeter song, and the sun to shine a golden yellow upon them all."

"That's nice," Vanessa said. "Turn the page."

Crystal snuggled closer to Claire. "Then what?"

"That's easy," Edwina replied. "Isn't it, Claire?"

The women shared a secret smile, then Claire turned the last page.

"And they lived happily ever after."

Seven children cheered.

COME FOR A VISIT—TEXAS-STYLE!

Where do you find hot Texas nights, smooth Texas charm and dangerously sexy cowboys? CRYSTAL CREEK!

This March, join us for a year in Crystal Creek...where power and influence live in the land, and in the hands of one family determined to nourish old Texas fortunes and to forge new Texas futures.

CRYSTAL CREEK reverberates with the exciting rhythm of Texas. Each story features the rugged individuals who live and love in the Lone Star State. And each one ends with the same invitation...

Y'ALL COME BACK...REAL SOON!

Watch for this exciting saga of a unique Texas family in March, wherever Harlequin Books are sold.

CC-G

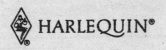

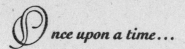

$\mathscr{O}$nce upon a time...

THERE WAS A FABULOUS
PROOF-OF-PURCHASE OFFER
AVAILABLE FROM

As you enjoy your Harlequin Temptation LOVERS & LEGENDS
stories each and every month during 1993, you can collect four
proofs of purchase to redeem a lovely opal pendant! The classic
look of opals is always in style, and this necklace is a perfect
complement to any outfit!

One proof of purchase can be found in the back pages of each
LOVERS & LEGENDS title . . . one every month during 1993!

LIVE THE FANTASY . . .

To receive your gift, mail this certificate, along with four (4) proof-of-purchase coupons from
any Harlequin Temptation LOVERS & LEGENDS title plus $2.50 for postage and handling (check
or money order—do not send cash), payable to Harlequin Books, to: **In the U.S.**: LOVERS &
LEGENDS, P.O. Box 9069, Buffalo, NY 14269-9069; **In Canada**: LOVERS & LEGENDS, P.O.
Box 626, Fort Erie, Ontario L2A 5X3.
Requests must be received by January 31, 1994.
Allow 4-6 weeks after receipt of order for delivery.

LLPOP-DIR

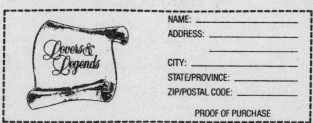

NAME: _____

ADDRESS: _____

_____

CITY: _____

STATE/PROVINCE: _____

ZIP/POSTAL CODE: _____

PROOF OF PURCHASE